Inky Quil

An eclectic collection from independent authors

Inky Quill Ramblings

Hope Community Library Creative Writing Group

First published in 2020

Copyright © Hope Community Library Creative Writing Group 2020

The rights of the authors have been asserted in accordance with Sections 77 and 78 of the Copyright Designs and Patents Act, 1988.

All rights reserved.
No part of this book may be reproduced (including photocopying or storing in any medium by electronic means and whether or not transiently or incidentally to some other use of this publication) without the written permission of the copyright holder except in accordance with the provisions of the Copyright, design and Patents Act 1988. Applications for the Copyright holder's written permission to reproduce any part of this publication should be addresses to the publishers.

ISBN: 9798646813849

This book is a work of fiction. Names, characters, businesses, organisations, places and events other than those clearly in the public domain, are either the product of the author's imagination or are used fictitiously. Any resemblance to actual persons, living or dead, events or locales is entirely coincidental.

Contributing authors have given non-time restricted permission to publish their work in this book.

Dedication

For Nigel, a former member and mentor who now watches us from above.

CONTENTS

Angelystor	11
Angharad	20
Black Dog	26
Devil's kitchen.	35
Cariad	36
Ceridwen	38
Chrwydryn	43
Feral Freda – a conversation	52
Gresford	54
Leeswood	59
Letters from a Country Gentleman	60
Look who's coming to dinner	77
No more words	84
Observation: A Slice of Farm Life	86
Sleeping Dragons	89
The Dinner Lady of Ysgol Newydd	91
The Hare and the eclipse.	96

Time to go.	99
Twm Golau	104
Ups and Downs	111
Wales Acrostic Poem	112
Y Ddraig Goch	113
About Hope Writing group	123
Biographies for Anthology	125

ANGELYSTOR

By D M Kelly

Welsh legend states that on the eve of the thirty-first day of the seventh and tenth month of the year, Angelystor, an ancient spirit who resides in a Yew tree in the local church yard, appears and announces the fate of those who will perish during the following year. Many believe it to be a dark fairy tale.

I know it to be true.

My quaint thatched cottage sits at the edge of the church yard, the oak framed sash windows overlooking the Yew tree, its stone walls partially covered in ivy and the garden filled with an array of colourful flowers which stand proud at the entrance. A stone path winds from the wooden slatted gate up to the intricately carved oak front door.

For such a beautiful cottage, people rarely notice it, or me. Only the unfortunate ones do. They look at me with blank expressions on their faces and an emptiness in their eyes. I smile at them and chuckle to myself as they walk by.

Every summer brings hippies and sun worshippers; autumn, witches and warlocks. There have even been a few so-called ghost hunters visiting. None of them find what they seek.

You would think they would learn. Angelystor only ever appears to the soul whose fate has been sealed. Those groups who seek the spirit out are mysteriously deterred before the black velvet darkness of the deepest night closes in.

Only when there is no audience at all, not even the church mice, only when the surrounding silence is more deafening than the wind that silently rushes through the gnarled branches of the old Yew tree, does Angelystor appear. The silence is eerie, even for me.

There is a moment that the silence reaches its peak, and you feel like you have gone completely deaf. This is the moment Angelystor leaves its lair from the masked exit of the 3000-year-old Yew Tree. You cannot see it unless you know where to look. A small dark patch of dead grass at the bottom of the stump where the exit meets the mossy grass of the church yard. Angelystor squeezes out, swirling around, opening the black layers of its ragged cloak, becoming wider and taller with every turn. Gathering momentum, finally freeing itself from the confines of its wooden prison, the spirit's floating arms spread out wide, the head flicking up as it unfurls to its full height. Angelystor remains almost still as it lingers in the air alongside the evergreen branches of the 3000-year-old tree.

The hour hand of the clock in the church

tower springs to midnight, but no chimes are heard. The eyes, mouth and cheekbones of the creature take on a distinct grey colouring, making its appearance even more frightening than before. It is then the boom of the voice comes. Deep, clear and loud. Only we can hear it, me and the unfortunate soul it has come to take.

It is a delight to see the realisation of where they suddenly find themselves. The puzzled look on their faces as the hypnotic gaze wears off. Eyes widening, jaw dropping and immense fear spreading across the whole face, draining the blood leaving a pale grey complexion. The whole body becoming rigid, arms tense up against their sides and fists clench leaving the skin over the knuckles white.

My favourite part is the hair, it is a spectacular sight. It works its way from the roots slowly. Changing from their natural colours to a sharp white, some even lose their hair. I wish I could be there when they see it for the first time. Their deaths vary greatly. Some meet their death within a few hours of leaving and others very nearly survive a year, although no one ever has. Each of them experiences either a freak accident or an unexplained illness. By the time their time comes, most of their mind has turned to a delightful mixture similar to frog spawn that has not quite set.

They leave quicker than they ever arrive. Looking back as they run, panting for breath and pulling at the grass in an attempt to pick themselves up having fallen in a feeble attempt to escape.

Angelystor looks over to me as always and gives a slight nod, having done its job and then disappears, far less dramatically than it arrived, back into the hollow of the Yew tree.

The following day is usually a good day for me. Everything seems brighter like a spring morning with dew sparkling on the grass as the sun rises and the birds sing in the tress. Over the years, this feeling has subsided, it's become stale. Even the delight of hearing the news of the recently deceased no longer holds the joy I once felt.

Perhaps it is time.

***

All Hallows Eve arrived. I gather my oils, candles, a cupful of fresh soil from the base of my beautiful Yew tree, plus a handful of its lovely leaves and a gnarly branch that had fallen naturally to the ground. My book waits in the hidden drawer of the old oak desk I use as my alter. I dress it with the deep violet, velvet cloth into which I've sewn the initials of all those who have perished. It has over 6000 sets of initials carefully sewn into it in an old Celtic scribe using gold thread for the women and silver for the men. I smooth the large cloth over the wooden surface allowing it to fall over all the sides and gather in pools of glistening fabric on the floor. I place the two intricately carved candle holders on either side of me and put the two church candles I have acquired from inside St Dygain's into position. I carefully set down the two smooth round stones that fit perfectly into the palm of each of my hands onto the alter. The gold offering plate sits in front of me.

My ritual has become ingrained into my brain. I do not really need to use the book for guidance, but its presence is just as much a part of the ritual as everything else. It also contains a secret ingredient that only I know and is hidden within the parchment pages of the thick, leather bound book.

Taking the book from the drawer in my desk, I run my hand over the worn cover and smile down at it. I place the book on its wrought iron stand to the side of me and carefully open it using the frayed red ribbon that has kept the page for so many years. The pages make a crinkling sound through years of use. As I open it, fragrances of earth, oils and smoke rise up and tickle the senses. I breathe them in deeply releasing a feeling of huge satisfaction. After a moment or two I remember the task I must perform. Tonight, is going to be a spectacular event.

Looking down at the pages, I find the beautiful first sprig of green I had taken from the Yew earlier in the year, more than enough to finish this year's harvest.

I take the sprig and place it on one of the stones. Picking them both up I grind them together while muttering the first part of my spell. As the moisture runs from the sprig down the stones and drips into the offering plate, I can smell the freshness of it. I scatter the soil from the ground onto the bright green liquid that has gathered in the centre of the plate. The oil is added before dropping in the leaves and stirring it with my ceremonial wooden ladle. After the last of leaves settle onto the mixture, I take a small piece of the branch and carefully whittle a few shavings of the bark in before grinding it altogether with the stones. It takes a while to get the texture right but working the mixture into a thick consistency is worth it. This seal needed to be strong.

As I work, I glance over through the window and see the wind is starting to rise, a slight tilt of my head allows me to see the clock face of the church, shining in the moonlight. It is almost time.

I continue with the ritualistic prayer, muttering it, not really saying it out loud. After lighting the candles, I lift one and gently tilt it over the mixture, allowing a small trickle of melted wax to flow onto the ingredients in the offering plate. I grab my fire tongs from beside the crackling, orange-glow fire and lift the plate from the table, placing it on the stone hearth in front of the fire so the wax remains soft. It can't set, not just yet. I grab a couple of logs from the wood basket and throw them on the fire. Picking up another log, I open the door of the old stove and throw it in, slamming the metal door shut before the logs can start spitting their shards of fiery wood at me. The copper kettle is sitting next to it, waiting its turn. I pick it up and place it on the only ring of the small stove and wait. Staring into the fire is so soothing and it helps me collect my thoughts for the events due to take place. It almost always fills me with joy, but this time, there is a peacefulness and an apprehension. Strange really. I knew this would come.

An unexpectedly loud crackle from the fire brings me back from my thoughts. I move everything from the altar so I can gather the cloth. I wrap it around me several times and drape it over my head like shawl, protecting me from the threatening storm. The kettle whistles to let me know the water is ready. I pour the water into a deep tin bowl and using the cloth, I pick the plate off the hearth and place it on top of it. It must not get cool.

As the hour nears midnight, I walk towards the tree, MY tree.

The silent storm engulfs me, the wind flowing through the cloth I have wrapped myself in. The spectacle is beginning. I have waited many years for this day, and it is finally upon me. As the clock strikes midnight, Angelystor begins to appear in its usual magnificent unfurling way. As Angelystor unfolds it suddenly looks down at me with an element of surprise on its striking face.

The moon appears from behind the dark grey clouds and the wind picks up even more, leaves and dust swirling. I place my plate on the ground before me and raise my arms up to the moon, repeating my prayer, out loud this time. My eyes wide and my smile broad as the sense of fear and disbelief moves over Angelystor's face as it clearly hears the name as he had with so many others.

"But do I not serve you well?" the voice

booms

"You do. You have, my faithful servant but I have grown tired now, older in years than any one mortal should, I must return to Him"

"But He will revoke me back to the fires"

"The Shawl of Souls will be presented to Him on my return. Each soul you have taken to keep me on this earth will transfer to Him and he will reward us both."

Angelystor knew it was bound to repeat the name of the next one to perish before the final chime of midnight. Angelystor knew the time had come. Like so many before, Angelystor was not ready.

As Angelystor reluctantly announces its own name, its form starts to disperse like smoke in the breeze. Angelystor's arm like forms grappling upwards towards the moon. Its head stretching, its features white with the fear it had instilled in others many times before. With one last reach and swirl of fear, the ancient spirit is gone just in time for the very last chime of midnight from the church tower.

In that moment, the storm is upon me. Thunder rolls; rain instantly falling onto me. I lift my still warm plate and walk to the entrance of Angelystor's lair and pour in the warm mixture. I watch it slowly solidify, sealing it.

As I walk slowly to my cottage, I turn to look at her. My faithful strong yew tree.

"Thank you, my trusted friend," I bow my

head in her direction and smile.

In that instant lightning strikes her right in her heart. My beautiful tree instantly engulfed in white hot flames quicker than I have ever seen before.

Shortly afterwards, I hear shouts coming from the nearby villagers, sirens as fire engines head this way. It would do no good – He had her now.

As I enter my home, I look around my curious cottage one last time and head to my bed. I lay down holding my book and the remaining sprig from my Yew, close my eyes and smile. The lighting comes one final time and strikes at the base of my precious yew tree, igniting the roots that have burrowed under my cottage and into its walls. The flames spread through them engulfing my home.

As the fire reaches me, the gathered souls leave my body groaning as they slip towards the ground, my body returns to its rightful age before the flames lap against my now tired, withered frame and with that, we are all gone.

***

Welsh legend states that an old witch lives in the cottage at the edge of the church. The villagers only see a beautiful young woman who spends her time caring for a sapling yew tree...

ANGHARAD

By Phil Burrows

Angharad changed the angle of her wings, allowing the wind to whisk her violently into the heavens. The light fluffy clouds deposited their moisture on leathery parts of her body, the wind forced the droplets backwards towards her tail, where they dispersed into a vapour trail. With a look full of devilment, Angharad pulled her wings in tight, enclosing her body, making it as sleek and as wind resistant as possible. She dropped, hurtling downwards with meteoric speeds, Angharad laughed as the heat from the friction caressed her. Counting her heart beats, the dragon gauged her descent and the distance between her and the ground below. At the last second, she thrust her mighty wings out, the exertion billowing them out like a silk parachute, breaking her fall.

The grey blanket of cloud and moisture swirled around the mountaintop as she flapped; with one out stretched talon she touched the peak of the mountain, leaving a small gouge, teasing it, as if to say *"You're not having me today"*.

Using a large spiraling motion, Angharad followed the air currents and with little effort she corkscrewed upwards, allowing the wind to perform the work for her. With her wings out wide, head and tail stretched she knew she looked sleek and graceful. Higher and higher she floated, until the clouds dispersed and the blue sky turning black, filled with twinkling gems. Holding her breath, she beat her wings to attain an even greater altitude; the air was becoming thinner and the water on her tail turned to ice. Her head wheeled with dizziness, her mind spinning as she fought for breath. Her muscles ached at the enormous effort and begrudgingly Angharad admitted defeat. She stopped flapping and turned over to watch the stars, with her chest heaving and her tired wings held out. Nature had not designed Dragons to fly upside down, not even in the best of conditions, at the height Angharad had attained, the air was too thin to support her weight. The rushing air brushed the ice off her tail as she fell. The stars faded, the sky became blue and eventually the clouds caressed her.

A grumbling noise in the distance interrupted her exuberance. Her eyes flared wide; it was humans in their infernal machines approaching. With a grunt and a flick of her tail, Angharad angled her body downwards, twisted and changed direction. Her heart raged at the intrusion as she plummeted into the clouds below.

Her natural chameleon abilities changed the colour of her skin as she left the open sky. Within seconds she became mottled with shades of white and grey, only her chest hinting at her location, nothing could truly hide the passionate red hues of her fiery heart. Gliding amongst the whispery water vapour, she waited for the deafening contraption to pass. Angharad snorted in defiance, small plumes of smoke billowing from her cavernous nostrils. *The food had become the hunter*; she thought.

Fearful of a second craft, Angharad calm herself by wallowing in a large and dense altocumulus. She grinned as she reminisced about times gone by, when the bipeds were nothing more than food and entertainment. How she and her family had laughed one day when they came across a light mortal floating in the heavens with the aid of trapped air and canvas. Her smile waned at the thought of the humans that flew now, encased inside metal containers, spewing rank odious fire from their rear. Angharad felt extra weary as on one occasion, the flying contraption had possessed had teeth that chased after her, gouging deep into the flesh when they struck each other. 'All things evolve and progress,' her mother had told her, 'to survive, we must adapt too.'

The clouds dispersed around her and she smiled at the sight below. She was flying above the craggy mountainous region the humans called Wales. A place of fluffy land clouds that bleated and wriggled as she whisked them off into the heavens. They were tasty snacks once she had burnt their hairy coats off. The Welsh mountains had once been a place full of her brethren. Where once she would have seen young dragons climbing the escarpments, she now saw the menacing bipeds swarming around the cliffs and peaks. The scenic valleys were full of them, crammed in their moving metal cans. All of them impatient, honking at each other like irate geese. Their anger boiled over, spoiling the tranquility of the mountain ranges. Angharad shook her head at the thought of the stupid parasitical lifeforms, so-called humanity. *Never mind*, she thought, she had evolved beyond their understanding now.

To the West she saw her home, with its green rolling hills and fertile ground that produced luscious vegetation. This nourished and sustained the plump meat creatures that she now preferred. Juicy and tender.

With eyesight that any hawk would be envious of, Angharad saw movement in her garden. Someone was in there, digging, a human. Food!

Stretching her long neck out, starting with a casual tilt of her head, Angharad angled her body towards her garden. Smiling to herself as she soared, the wind whistled through her claws as she opened and closed them in anticipation. Her vision narrowed as she drew closer, the blue of the oceans gone from her periphery. Soon the greys of the mountain range disappeared too, until she could only see the vibrant greens of her fields. Further down she flew. There was, after all, no need for her to slow down, she was a dragon, a creature of magic and fire. With her impeccable sight, she watched the man till the earth, turning it over, one spade full at a time. Beads of sweat formed on his bald head as he worked, growing larger until gravity pulled them down onto the human's forehead and eyes.

Angharad's body began to change now, she could not allow a human to see her natural form. Where there is one biped, there are always more. Her skin, momentarily blue and white to blend in with the clouded sky above, began to change. Her legs shortened; her neck drew back into her shoulders. Her fire filled chest shrank, though the vibrancy of her flame never diminished.

Angharad's stomach rumbled as she watched the tasty morsel below. Brown bare skin glistening in the sun. Her mouth salivated as the aroma of her next meal wafted upwards to meet her. With legs down and claws out at the ready, she swooped.

The human looked up, startled at the movement, shielding his eyes from the sun's mighty incandescence, he stared as Angharad landed beside him. Her sharp claws sinking into her meal, it writhed and fought for escape before she gobbled it whole.

Looking at the man, she tweeted in appreciated and began to preen her newly grown feathers, all the time searching for another feast. Her breast flamed red as nothing could truly hide the magical fire within.

She pounced as the man turned over another spade full of soil and having retrieved her dinner, flew to perch on the handle of a garden fork, a fat wriggling worm in her beak.

BLACK DOG

By Eileen O'Reilly

Stuart found the holiday caravan online. The reviews were good and there was a pub serving food a short walk away, so he booked it. He mentioned it to his counsellor at their next session.

'And how do you feel about it now?'

'One minute I'm all right with it – taking it as a sign that the depression is under control – the next, I feel sick at the thought of riding the bike, though it's a journey I've made many times.'

'But not since the accident?'

'No. Not since then.'

'You don't have to do this, you know. It takes time.'

'I do, or I never will.'

***

Stuart rode into the café car park and pulled the bike onto its stand. He'd taken it slow and easy, setting off after the morning rush had died down, and was pleased to find his new bike had handled the winding narrow roads of North Wales with ease.

His confidence had grown with every mile

travelled; his body reacting instinctively to the twists and turns, eyes scanning ahead for danger. He felt *alive*.

He left his bike helmet on a picnic table, saving the seat while he placed his order. When he returned, a woman sat there, a black dog sprawled at her feet.

'I hope you don't mind sharing? Only Gwyllgi gets a bit anxious in crowds and this table is out of everyone's way. My partner's gone to get us something to eat.'

Mindful of his counsellor's advice that he try to be more sociable, Stuart leaned down and scratched behind the dog's floppy ears. One of its back legs twitched.

'Gwilgee?'

'*Gwyllgi*. It's Welsh for black dog.' The dog stretched and yawned, showing sharp teeth. Stuart pulled his hand back.

'And what breed is he?'

'Well that's the mystery, *isn't it Gwyl*? A bit of Wolfhound in there we think, possibly Great Dane. Gwyn, my partner, jokes that he's part wolf, part elephant, but we wouldn't have him any other way. *No we wouldn't, would we?*' The dog thumped its tail and stared at Stuart, licking its lips. Its eyes were an unusual shade of reddish-brown. The dog growled, a low rumble deep in its throat; Stuart was the first to look away.

Stuart had finished his bacon bap when a man approached the table with a tray and quickly laid out drinks and four burger boxes. He sat down and nodded to Stuart then began speaking to the woman in Welsh. She nodded and unwrapped a burger from its box, broke it into half and placed it on the floor in front of the dog.

Jaws snapped and the burger disappeared. The dog rested its massive head on its paws and closed its eyes.

'Just out for the day are you?' The man took a bite of his burger and chewed.

'On holiday. I've booked a caravan for a few days. Can't go in until three o'clock though. How about you? Local are you?'

'You could say that. We move around a bit, but we always come back. No place like home, eh, Mattie?'

'Home is where the heart is, Gwyn.'

'So they say, *cariad*. So they say.' He unwrapped the last burger and fed it to the dog, who swallowed it whole, sniffing the floor for more food scraps then rested its head on its paws once more and stared at Stuart. Its red eyes gave him the heebie-jeebies

Stuart had eaten everything apart from some bacon rind but he picked it up and the dog opened its mouth wide for him to drop it in. Its breath stank. Stuart coughed and turned away.

'Sorry, I should have warned you about that.' The woman wiped her hands on her clothes. 'He's got an infected tooth. I've been treating him myself; we prefer natural methods, herbs and hedgerow plants. It's working, but slowly.'

Now Stuart looked at her properly, he saw that her dark hair showed silvery strands in the sunlight and her skin was tanned with a few freckles dotted over her nose. She wore a long dress, its pattern faded, and tiny silver bangles jingled on both arms when she moved her hands. Neon-pink flip-flops drew his attention to her grubby feet.

Her companion wore a blue and pink striped cotton tunic over red corduroy trousers. A sage-green velvet waistcoat and brown sandals completed the look. The man even had a gold earring peeping out from tangled grey curls. His face was thin, etched with deep lines, yet there was a mischievous twinkle in his sapphire-blue eyes. Stuart downed his last mouthful of sweet black coffee.

'Well, I'd better make a move. Nice to meet you both, and Gwyllgi, of course. I hope his tooth is better soon.'

'You take care now. These roads can be lethal for bikers; they ride too fast and don't see the bends until it's too late. We've seen the aftermath, haven't we *cariad*?'

'Poor souls. Didn't know what hit them, did they?'

'Thanks for the warning.' Stuart picked up his helmet and walked away. Three pairs of eyes, one pair now a deep red, watched him walk away.

He used the facilities then wandered into the shop. He bought a crusty loaf, bacon, sausages, mushrooms and half-a-dozen eggs; breakfast for the next few days. Welsh whisky would be his nightcap.

A mate had poured him a glass last Christmas and he'd enjoyed it enough to want to try it again.

Lunch would be whatever he picked up as he travelled around the area; dinner - whatever the pub had to offer, along with a pint of the local beer. He never drank to excess, and never when riding the bike, but one pint and one small whisky wasn't going to kill him, and he'd stick to soft drinks on his final night.

At the checkout, he picked up a book of local myths and legends, on sale for half the price on the cover, and bought it. He hadn't thought to bring anything to read, so this would be just the thing. He would leave it in the caravan for the next visitors.

Mattie and Gwyn drove past as he walked back to the bike. He'd had them down for a VW camper or a converted bus or ambulance, but their choice of vehicle was way beyond what he had imagined. With Mattie in the passenger seat and Gwyl curled up in the back, Gwyn carefully manoeuvred a dark-purple hearse towards the exit, indicating to turn right. Stuart packed his purchases into a pannier and rode off in the opposite direction, towards Bala.

Stuart decided to carry on into the town and buy a hot pie for his lunch before parking up by the lakeside.

His parents had always headed for Llangower Station on family days out. As a teenager, he'd thought the place boring and desolate, but still felt a secret boyish thrill as the narrow-gauge engines steamed by. Revisiting old haunts appealed to him today.

On Sunday outings, his father had often struggled to find a space to park and resorted to parking on the grass verge, making an already narrow road even trickier for other drivers. Today, on a weekday and with school holidays not due to start for a few weeks, there was only one car in the tiny car park. Stuart put the bike up on its stand and grabbed his lunch and the myths and legends book.

It was pleasantly warm on the lakeshore with the sun beating down. He'd eaten his pie and read a few chapters of his book before stretching out on the long seat of the picnic table and closing his eyes. He slept soundly, for once, waking only when the distant whistle of an approaching train sounded.

Dark clouds had drifted in and a cold breeze ruffled the surface of the water. The lake-shore had changed, becoming the desolate place of his childhood memories. Stuart binned his rubbish and strode towards the gate that accessed the railway and car park beyond.

The whistle sounded much closer now. He fancied he could hear his mother's voice as it had been when he was a young boy. *Don't cross the line, Stuart. Wait for the train to pass.*

Across the line, a woman in a flowing dress stepped onto the opposite platform, a large black dog at her side. She resembled Mattie, but appeared much older. Her hair was white and dishevelled, tendrils blowing about in the breeze like writhing snakes. Her face gaunt and wrinkled, she staggered as if about to collapse and Stuart took a step forward to go and help her.

Don't go to her Stuart. Once more he heard his mother's voice. *The train is coming. She isn't who you think she is. Don't look at the dog.*

Stuart looked anyway. Gwyllgi stood almost as tall as Mattie, the silhouette of a beast, almost invisible against a darkening sky. A shadow. A phantom with eyes of glowing red: eyes that goaded him to cross the line. *Look away Stuart. The train is coming. Don't cross.*

With a squeal of brakes, the engine came to a juddering stop. Steam hissed. Water dripped. Two passengers climbed out from one of the cramped carriages onto the platform. They took photographs as the guard blew his whistle and waved his flag. The train steamed away towards Bala. The old woman and the black dog opposite had gone.

Stuart followed the passengers to the car park and retrieved his helmet and gloves. It couldn't have been Mattie he'd seen, nor his mother's voice he'd heard. She been dead for twelve years, his dad for fifteen.

Maybe he'd been dreaming about his parents, the familiar scenery tickling buried memories. But that didn't explain Mattie's changed appearance. She and Gwyn had been friendly, though that dog of theirs was a monster for all its ear scratches and belly rubs. And the stench from its gaping mouth. He shivered. He was glad that he hadn't mentioned to the couple exactly *where* he'd be staying.

He took the back roads to the farm. The caravan was ready for him and the owner, Seren, said she'd left a welcome pack for him.

'It's just milk and butter, some home-made jam and scones. Give me a knock if you need anything else, otherwise I'll leave you to find your own way.'

The caravan was tucked away behind the farm and couldn't be seen from the road. It was perfect.

He made himself a coffee topped up with whisky, then sat at the small table. He still felt shaken. When Mattie and the dog had appeared out of thin air, he'd felt an overwhelming compulsion to step off the platform right in front of the little train.

And hearing his mum's voice warning him? She was dead. He'd watched her die, yet he had heard her voice quite clearly, as though she was stood next to him. He must have been dreaming; a combination of hot weather and the stress of getting back on a bike again, that's all. He'd read for a bit, then go to the pub for an early dinner.

He couldn't find his 'myths' book; must have left it behind at the picnic site. He wasn't going to go back to look for it though. Fortunately, the caravan was well stocked with books, including a copy of the latest Dan Brown. He buttered a couple of scones and began to read.

The *Myths and Legends* book lay where he'd left it, on the table. The wind ruffled its pages yet it fell open at the same place each time.

> ***The Gwyllgi*** *is a mythical dog of Welsh legend with the appearance of a mastiff or black wolf. It is said to have glowing red eyes and 'baleful' breath. A portent of death, the hound is often accompanied by an ancient hag known as Matilda of the night.*

DEVIL'S KITCHEN.

By Mair Dunlop

Deep dark crevices,
Towering, encased in cloud,
Rolling hills infest,
No further can be seen,
Than those that stand before,
Leaving a languishing rebound.

CARIAD

(in living memory of Louis)
By Susanne Allcroft

The sweetest heart I've ever known,
my little dyn bach annwyl
He follows me throughout my days,
we're side by side until,
The gentle paw-fall on the carpet,
followed by a sigh,
His "nos da" just a kindly lick 'fore gentle
snores are nigh.
To find me every door is nudged by
wet nose or black pad,
His brown eyes seek to share my
thoughts, my loving cariad.

This sweetest heart has walked with
me for miles to pen-y-bryn,
Through greenest woods we've wandered
long, swam through the coldest llyn,
A loyal friend, companion true,
he's there to be my shield,
A tilted head to check my mood,
my hurt is always healed

A confidant who doesn't judge,
feel anger or get mad,
Just fierce allegiance, loyal trust, my loving cariad.

We've shared our food, a bed and
chair, whatever's his is mine,
We've joined our worlds together,
our spirits they align,
I understand just what he wants, he's
there when life's a muddle,
A paw to proffer, reassures me, offers me a cuddle.
A better friend throughout my life
I never could have had,
My dyn bach annwyl, right hand
dog, my loving cariad.

CERIDWEN
By P N Burrows

A shaft of early morning sunlight pierced through the rain-filled clouds, they had yet to decide if they would disperse their water on the ragged mountainous peaks below. The thin beam of light glittered as it passed through the thinning fog. Halos made from sparkling rainbows formed as the sunbeam danced across a small section of the jagged precipice. The mountain groaned as if in protest, small stones stirred, pools of fine grit rippled like water in the wind and nesting birds squawked in alarm as they flew away.

The loud crack of shattering rock rang out across the Welsh valley, echoing in the distance, disturbing more birds from their far away perches. Huge slabs of rock broke away from the cliff face, falling with calamity as they rebounded off the escarpment below.

Ceridwen opened her eyes, alert but unsure of what had awoken her, she remained still and listened.

The wind whipped across her face, her cheeks

were as cold as ice. The chill of the Welsh mountain range was a summer breeze compared to the frozen tundra that Ceridwen grew up in. Not wanting to move, lest she spoil her comfortable sleeping position for naught, she strained her eyes left and right. She could just make out the slumbering forms of her family and companions, feeling safe among them she started to drift off, back to sleep. It's too early to be awake, much too early she thought with dismay. Hearing nothing, she began to doze once more. In a semi-conscious, half dream like state Ceridwen's leg twitched, rousing herself once more and dislodging a handful of loose shale, the stones clattered down the cliff face, breaking the peaceful silence. Dozing, Ceridwen had dreamed of snow and ice, crystal white vistas for as far as her eyes could see, a frozen sparkling tundra of delight. Her home.

A strange sound rose from the depths, carried on the wind, ethereal, a whisper of garbled nonsense. Ceridwen's eyes widened. Alert now, she listened. After a short while, a repetitive tapping echoed, followed by more unfathomable animal noises, they sounded shrill and anxious. Ceridwen stirred slightly causing more shale and rock to fall. The animals below squawked and became agitated. Whatever they were, they were climbing up the cliff face, something was about to trespass on her family's escarpment.

Small creatures, she thought, her head clear now, the grogginess of sleep having evaporated at the thought of interlopers. She could smell the animals now, their warm bodies were perspiring in fear.

Something climbed upon her toes, the tapping sound occurred once more and she felt a sharp sting as something sharp forced its way into her skin. She could smell the metallic tang of steel in the air, with each hammer blow the essence of iron increased around her. A minute later another metallic spike was pounded into the craggy folds of her knee.

Small like the wolves of old, she assured herself, but animals don't use metal, she frowned in confusion, her brow creaking loudly as she did so.

Reluctantly Ceridwen tilted her head slowly forwards to see down, along her body. Two strange creatures clad in multihued colours of red and orange clung to her craggy thighs.

'Earthquake!' one of the animals shouted.

The words were meaningless to Ceridwen, a jabber of nonsense carried on the wind. The creatures scaled higher, frantic to reach the top before another landslide dislodged them from the cliff face.

Ceridwen groaned, a rock filled mountainous rumble of a sound at the intrusion. 'It's too early to wake, it's too warm!' she moaned. Ceridwen was dismayed as she looked around, there was no ice on the peaks, no glaciers in the valley. 'It not morning yet!' she roared in annoyance. The crack and rumble of her words reverberated down the valleys.

The next ice age was still far away, and she

was so very tired.

The lone shaft of light moved across her lichen covered companions as the clouds moved southwards. It briefly illuminated Ceridwen's creased and rugged face. She was considered beautiful by her peers. In the morning the young males would woo her, and babies would follow, maybe as many as three broods before the glaciers began to melt and the long slumber between ice ages befell the trolls once more.

The climbing animals drove a metal peg into her chest, a nuisance nothing more, the small creatures could not really harm her, except for sleep deprivation she mused. She was of rock and stone, a goliath compared to these two tiny creatures. They huddled for a moment in the crevasse of her bosom, gesturing wildly to one another, arms flailing around as they planned their ascent. One pointed to the left of Eta's head, the other right, neither liking the fact that the large rock outcrop was leaning downwards, facing directly at them.

Clenching her chest muscles together Ceridwen closed the space between her pert stone breasts. The groaning sound of her bouldery mammaries, grinding the trespassers into paste drowned out their pitiful, high-pitched screams.

'Sleep, just need to sleep.' Ceridwen whispered as she pushed herself deeper into the rock face, the strata and her body becoming one. The chill of the mountain was comforting while the warmth of the Welsh winter lulled Ceridwen into closing her heavy eyes lids, the thought of the next ice age brought a smile to her face as she fell asleep.

CHRWYDRYN

By Mair Dunlop

"What have you got in there" Anne asked Val, pointing at the Spar bag in her left hand when they met outside the chapel.

"Bread, milk, tea bags, French Fancies - they were on offer £1 a box!"

"You've brought your shopping to a funeral, oh my goodness Val, that's shocking"

"Why?" Val responded with a confused 'what's the problem' kind of look on her face.

"It's hardly the 'done thing' is it? Anne quipped, rolling her eyes in distain"

"Ah don't be so dramatic Anne, it's not like anyone will notice! I bet we are the only ones here anyhow. Besides it's a fitting tribute, she always carried a Spar bag." Val defended her choice whilst making herself as comfortable as she could on the carved wooden bench, the words 'on the setting of the sun, we will remember them' still etched deeply along the top wooden slat yet the name to remember beneath it now worn away on a tarnished bronzed plaque.

Feral Freda, the local tramp, had been nicknamed many years ago by some local kids. The name had stuck and so did she, living rough in the village. She sometimes wandered out of the local area to a neighbouring town or two but she always returned to Cefn-y-Caer. That's where she was found; stiff and cold amongst the yellow daffodils in the graveyard, her dirt black, grimy, pale face had the matt blank empty shell look that only comes with death.

Freda was known to all but a few, yet her substance was not known to any. She spoke to no-one, with the exception of the odd obscene collection of swear words usually hurled at the local youths who found her fascinating and followed her around occasionally with intrigue and trepidation! The adrenaline rush fed such behaviour, as the incessant teasing often resulted in an angry chase erupting from Freda. The only peace she found from bouts of such taunts were during the winter months and term times when the "youths" were otherwise contained within their homes or educational institutions. She knew she scared them half to death, her dirty face and stooped over posture exaggerated by the weight of an off cut piece of carpet that she carried around with her; something to lay on the ground and sleep on presumably, a much needed barrier between her and the hard, damp, cold and stony earth. But where did she sleep? No-one was ever sure but often remnants of small fires would be found down lanes, in derelict buildings, within the local church grounds. There were, however, no ashes where she had last laid down, and no off cut carpet, just a plastic carrier containing within it what little she owned, a worn leather pouch and striped woollen scarf, the colours now just various shades of brown. Who she really was and why she was the way she was had remained a mystery, yet the numerous theories on her existence were often discussed by the locals over a pint, over a fence, in the local café.

Anne sat down next to Val with such a force that the slats beneath Val's bottom creaked.

"Told me to piss off once you know!" Val exclaimed "I only offered her a box of Mr Kipling's. Come to think of it they were French Fancies, she growled under her breath then shuffled off"

"I would have told you to piss off if you offered me a French Fancy. Awful bloody things. I don't know why you like them so much." Anne quipped, again.

"I don't know why I like them, the fondant is a bit sickly sweet but I do like the bleached white, soft sponge and besides, they remind me of being a little girl, birthday parties, picnics on long summer days and all that" Val defended.

"She led such a sad existence." A look of honest sadness was apparent on Anne's face.

"A sad existence you say, I guess so, but there was no need to be so, so rude to people. Remind me Anne why are we here again?" Val questioned.

"Oh Val, we might be the only ones who are here, that's why I wanted to come. I couldn't stand the thought of her having no-one here at the end to say goodbye"

Val thought she could see a tear in Anne's eye as she empathised with her friend "I felt sorry for her too but she didn't help herself much did she?"

A helping hand was regularly offered to Freda from all the appropriate avenues, Salvation Army, the local convent, the constabulary, but she never freely accepted, the exception being those times when she was unable to refuse, episodes of ill health and during the cold and bitter times of the deep mid-winter. As soon as she could though she was back out treading the tarmac barefoot in summer and in oversized men's boots in winter.

"We better go in Val and take a seat, the Vicars coming, whereby shall we sit?"

"The bloody back!" Val responded.

"Morning Vicar," both Anne and Val chimed at the same time as they took their place halfway up the aisle, near the back, hidden by a stone pillar. Before any further conversation could be commenced between the three, a solitary figure emerged just outside the church doors adorned in black, acceptable funeral attire. The Vicar scurried over and placed his hand on the shoulder of this particular female. Her hair was perfectly tied up in a French knot and her face adorned with a pair of large dark designer sunglasses. The vicar offered her a tissue which she gratefully received and used it to wipe her eyes beneath. Quickly, behind her, three young men and then three more middle aged men arranged themselves. Neither Val nor Anne recognised any of these figures, although it was hard to see them properly as the glaring early summer sun was streaming through the large, arched doorway. The vicar caught hold of the female figure's elbow and gently moved her aside, then a coffin parted the six men from behind, they lifted it to their shoulders and commenced up the aisle as the deep gut-stirring organ music began to play.

"Who do you think they are, Anne? I didn't think she had any family, well, family that cared anyhow," Val whispered to her dear friend, "and look, there are more of them," the shock evident in her voice as half a dozen younger individuals followed behind the coffin past Anne and Val.

A congregation of 13 individuals made up the funeral party, not including Anne and Val, all of various ages from early 20s upwards. It was presumed by the two women that these were the female's husband, children and grandchildren as it certainly appeared that she was the matriarch of them all and a familiarity was evident in some form or another amongst members of the congregation. The female's tear-stained face and the genuinely sad aura that surrounded her when she passed by, walking up the aisle, left Anne and Val feeling very much out of place like two interfering 'busy bodies' there for a good old nose. The organ music ended abruptly and the shuffling of feet, bags and bodies all finding their place on the pews was all that could be heard, then stillness came with the commencement of prayers.

"Amen." the Vicar concluded.

"Amen." reverberated the funeral party, Anne and Val.

The matriarch woman got up and walked towards the parapet and out of her Burberry handbag with a shaking hand she took out a folded-up piece of A4 paper. She placed her bag on the floor, unfolded the parchment, had a small cough to clear her throat and started to speak.

"Freda, old Norse for beautiful and beloved. This is perhaps not how some would have seen my elder and only sister, but I did. As a child she was my protector, my teacher and my rock. We had an uncertain upbringing created by the comings and goings of many a father figure, our real father having died when we just knee high to a grasshopper. The others that came and went after were a myriad of characters, all abusive in differing ways, none nurturing, loving or kind, none of them even close to the father we had lost. Our mother could not see, as her pain relief for the deep grief she felt was found at the bottom of a gin bottle or two. She lost her beloved husband, Richard, so young in life. Yet she was lucky, she had found such pure love in her life – they were, after all, childhood sweethearts but the loss of him tore her apart. She was left unable to function in the day to day world. She tried to seek solace with the men she found in the local pub, trying to fill an emotional void and who could blame her?"

A moment passed whilst Freda's sister sipped

from a glass of water, finding the strength to continue with her eulogy. Anne and Val felt a discomfort which had descended around them;

"Shall we go?" Anne whispered to Val.

"We can't go now and this was your idea, remember, we're staying," Val whispered back with the voice of authority.

"Freda was a clever girl and found the skills required to help us survive such a rollercoaster upbringing very quickly. She had, however, developed a mistrust of all, she did not easily accept help after being stung so many times by false offerings of assistance. Never a helping hand was given without having a repercussion associated to it. In the black of night when power cuts were frequent, often a beast would come to disturb what should have been our safe haven. Freda took the brunt of such treatments and would hide me away in a wardrobe or under a bed. Not once did I see her cry but so often she was a shoulder for me to cry on, she would stroke my hair and reassure me that one day, one day we would be free. She promised me that she would save us and that we could run away to live together, to be safe and to be happy. Many a night we would plan our escape and talk about what our future lives could be like. She loved to write, poetry being a particular strength, she found escapism, happiness and joy in the written word. Her ambition was to be an author but unfortunately her dream was not to become her reality".

An uncomfortable silence hung in the air of

the church, Anne and Val sat still and quiet. Both knowing that the other was also feeling a great weight of shock, sadness, sorrow and discomfort for these two young girls who had endured such an upbringing that was a world away from their own.

The woman continued, a quiver in her voice and silent tears running down her face streaking the matt black mascara from her eyelashes hidden away beneath the ' Coco channel' designer sunglasses.

"As a young woman, Freda had worked in bars and pubs, never touching a drop of the poison that had caused such chaos in our lives and had taken our mother away from us. We had fled our home as soon as we could and never returned. Both of us worked hard to ensure that we could live, to support each other, although she always worked harder than me. I am ashamed to say I took advantage of her. She struggled to find a partner, someone to love, despite trying many times and having many an admirer, for she was a beautiful young woman, her dark auburn hair would shine and her eyes were bright green like two pieces of sea glass. When I left our home to marry, although she would never admit it, I do believe I broke her heart. This for me is the hardest part, I blame myself for her life that followed. She struggled to support herself mentally, physically and financially but never did she tell me, never did she ask for help. She distanced herself and, blinded to this through love and marital bliss, I had presumed that she was jealous of my happiness. I had abandoned her, left her to fend for herself. After all she was the strong one, the one who was the fighter, the one who was tough. Without me though, without me to look after her, I do believe she was lost, lonely and forgotten. She led her middle years on the streets, unable to accept help, refusing anything that was offered to her, always distrusting of everyone. Ten years after I had left her, left our home, I finally found the courage to go and find her and when I did, it broke my heart. I tried many times to bring her back to me, to my home, to be safe and to be loved but I failed every time. All I could do was try and support her in the life she was living. Not wanting to be a hindrance, she had once again sacrificed herself, her life for me. Today is the saddest day of my life, as I can no longer keep trying to save her, to bring her home to be with me, to be with my family, her family. Now she is gone and I am so very sorry that I didn't succeed, that I could not save her the way she saved me."

Anne and Val quietly left the church during a hymn, the beautiful sound of Amazing Grace drifting away behind them as they walked away. They had not spoken, had not looked at each other all the way back to Anne's House.

"Cup of tea Val?"

"Yes please, white with sugar." replied Val.

"Of course, would you like a plate for your French Fancy?"

"No ta Anne, I don't quite fancy one at the moment".

FERAL FREDA – A CONVERSATION

By Mair Dunlop and Nigel Johnson

On Thursday May 31st 2018, Mair Dunlop (pseudonym), a member of Hope Community Library Creative Writing Group, wrote to Nigel Johnson, a fellow member of the creative writing club, professor of English, playwright and critic:

"Good Evening Nigel

I have attached my story about Feral Freda so you could see how it ended. It's not the cheeriest read I am afraid!

Kind Regards

Mair"

His reply, on Saturday June 2nd 2018,

"Hi Mair

Have received your Feral Freda opus.. Many thanks. Look forward to reading it and will be in touch

All the best

Nigel"

Then:

"Hi Mair

Have read your story. You're right…. not the happiest of sagas but it definitely works. The fondant fancies prove a very powerful image, representing a careless happy childhood that cannot be readily related to, leading to an effectively abrupt ending. Great stuff!

Was watching a report on the current tennis tournament and came across the name Tatiana. Lovely name for a down-and-out woman…. Tatty Anna, Sorry! Russian, perhaps? But I do like Feral Freda.

Thanks again for the story.

Nigel"

Nigel was a highly intelligent wordsmith with a great imagination and sense of humour who could always be relied upon to give constructive and positive criticism of others' writing. He is greatly missed.

GRESFORD

Eileen O'Reilly

They came from miles around. Solemn-faced men in worn jackets; bewildered women clutching tear-stained handkerchiefs, some with babes in arms. Silent children with sleep in their eyes and bed-ruffled hair.

They stand in uneven rows along the fences, or on the shifting scree of spoil heaps. Wherever a gap opens up, someone shuffles forwards or sideways to close it. Their silhouettes against the grey skyline are as black as the coal beneath their feet. Those who can, pray, though they know it will take more than faith and prayer to save lives on this day.

Empty coal trucks remain in the sidings; their usual cargo of coal exchanged for a human one as men from other pits arrive to stand vigil for their missing comrades. The name *Gresford* painted two-feet high on the side of every one. A name that will become famous. A name that will be infamous. A name that will inspire poetry, song and protest.

Rain has been falling since first light. It carves deep lines in the coal-black faces of the rescuers as they wait their turn to descend the shaft again.

Lowered on a bosun's chair – thick rope and a plank of wood to sit on; feet in their heavy boots crossed at the ankles so they don't scrape the sides of the shaft and make sparks. One hand resting on the chain of the lift to stop them spinning on the descent.

The rescuers change places at the shaft bottom. No time for chat, just the fleeting glimpse of a head bowed in despair, the white flash of eyes against a black face, the brief touch of a hand on a stooped shoulder, before the chair ascends once more into the light.

Each exhausted rescuer returns with the same story. **HEAT. FIRE. GAS.** Three words which completely fail to capture the inferno that rages below; has been raging for seven hours or more since the initial explosion in the small hours, when a tremor shook the ground above; rattling windows and crockery, set sleeping dogs howling; causing fear and dread in the hearts of the families above.

Volunteers are lowered each in their turn. No-one refuses. One man goes down, one comes up. None wear breathing apparatus. All have the courage of lions.

Any survivors?

Each time a shake of the head. They have no breath with which to answer. No words to describe the horror underground where fire rages like the very pits of Hell and the rock face cracks and fragments as they crawl on hands and knees like penitents before a wrathful God.

A man pushes to the front of the queue eager to take his turn, but he is led away. They will not ask this of *him*. Not today.

Six of them got out. Pulled at the jagged rocks with their bare hands and crawled through gaps no bigger than a shovel's width. Climbed the ladders all the way, then ran like hell. See the bloody bandages on his hands? He's worn them to the bone, they say.

How many left down there?

No-one knows yet.

I've heard there could be a hundred or more.

I've heard two hundred.

Some were working a double shift, so they could go to the match today.

Everyone in the Martin shaft got out. Felt the explosion right through the soles of their boots and legged it.

Diolch i Grist.

All that day, and the next, people wait for news. Rumours spread that the miners are safe. But none appear. Each attempt by the rescue parties to clear the rock falls only feeds the flames. Carbon monoxide levels are so high that miners who escaped the fireball will have perished within minutes.

The decision is made.

A murmur runs through the crowds. Caps are removed. Heads bow in defeat. The women, wives and mothers who have waited stoically for news of their men, surrender to their pain and grief.

They're withdrawing the rescue parties. Leaving

our brothers to their fate.

Bastardiaid! They've known for years about the firedamp in that section. Never did anything about it.

The owners should be prosecuted. And the deputies that did their dirty work, pushing productivity, knowing it wasn't safe.

Murderers! They'll get away with it though, you'll see.

They always do.

***

Two-hundred-and-sixty-two miners lost their lives on that fateful 24th September 1934; the oldest was 67, the youngest aged just 15. Three rescuers also died, and one surface worker was killed later when the cap blew off one of the shafts. Eleven bodies were recovered, leaving two-hundred-and fifty-four men sealed in their underground tomb forever.

The inquiry into the disaster opened one month later, on 25 October, in Wrexham. Management failures, lack of safety measures, bad working practices and poor ventilation in the pit were all highlighted as contributing to the loss of life.

Gresford Colliery reopened six months after the disaster with coal production resuming in January 1935, before finally closing in November 1973. The Dennis section was never re-opened.

In 2014, an application to extract coal-bed gas by drilling or 'fracking' was turned down by the local authority, though their decision was later overruled by the Welsh Assembly Government. However, since September 2018, Welsh Government policy is that no new licences will be granted for fracking, and those with existing licences will be required to apply for consent or approval before work can commence.

LEESWOOD

By Margaret Arndt

Many a winding road
On looking to Moel Famau
And over to Padeswood.

Down the paths I would go
Blackberry picking
Minding my fingers
On the brambles in
The wood.

The Nant would
Traverse up to Leeswood.

LETTERS FROM A COUNTRY GENTLEMAN

Eileen O'Reilly

> Erddig Hall
> 26th May 1733

Dear Cousin Philip,

I thank you for your kind letter of condolence regarding our late uncle John Meller and your good wishes towards myself and my wife now our fortunes have changed.

You generously inquired into my plans for the Estate and I have some news regarding renovations to the House which you may find of interest.

We are comfortably settled in our new home after some weeks of disarray, and my thoughts have turned to how best to enhance the House in a style more suited to my improved status. I am minded to decorate at least one room using the new wall paper, which you yourself have mentioned with great admiration on several occasions, and I have determined that the large bedroom above the front portico will fit my purpose well. I believe you will recall that particular room from your own visits.

After much correspondence with my Agent in London, I have secured the services of a reputable printer and purveyor of wall papers, called Perriman. Perhaps you know of him? My architect has provided him with all the necessary details of the room, including measurements and sketches, and in turn he has despatched samples of the papers that I may make my choice.

I have taken a fancy to a pattern in the Chinese style, consisting of a coloured background overlaid with a fretwork of delicate tree branches on which perch a number of exotic birds. But here's the rub. If I purchase ready printed wall paper, then the exorbitant sum of one shilling per square yard must be paid to Treasury coffers for this pernicious wall paper tax. If I purchase rolls of plain paper, there is no requirement to pay the tax. The trick then is to purchase the plain paper. Thus I am forced into duplicity and subterfuge in order to avoid additional expense. But I am determined to have my desire and, therefore, would ignore the pricking of my conscience.

Two or three artisans are to accompany the paper on its journey. They will first hang the paper, then draft the pattern directly onto the wall and finally apply the paint. The men will require bed and board while they complete the task but that will be but a paltry amount; and I will have sufficient funds in hand to decorate the finished room with appropriate fixtures and furnishings of a similar style.

I believe this to be a most favourable outcome, and one-in-the-eye for the Excise Men who seek only to relieve me of my hard earned guineas. In addition, by completing the decoration *in situ,* the quality of my wall paper will far exceed that seen in the richer homes and salons of London where, you have told me, the pattern does not always match as precisely as it should.

I trust this letter finds you in continued good health.

>Your cousin
>>Simon Y-------

12th August, 1733

Dear Philip,

Thank you for your inquiries on my behalf regarding Mister Perriman. It is exceedingly gratifying to know that I have chosen a man with such an excellent reputation for artistry and design among London's *haut-monde.*

It has been some little time since the artisans from London commenced their labours on my behalf and the decoration of the Chinese bedroom is almost complete. The entire process fascinated me from the moment it began.

Mr Perriman himself had accompanied his men to deliver the paper and other appurtenances, declaring himself greatly taken with the sketches provided and expressing a wish to see the room, and indeed the remainder of the House, for himself. Anticipating my eagerness to have the decorations completed swiftly, Perriman explained he had recently perfected a system used by the French, which would greatly expedite the initial pattern transfer; he showed me an offcut of paper to demonstrate his purpose. I could immediately discern his intentions and gave my wholehearted agreement for him to proceed.

After a night's rest and a frugal breakfast, he and his men assembled in the empty room where they prepared the necessary which would allow them to fix the paper to the bare plaster walls. I regret to report that the noxious fumes which emanated from their preparations became too much for me and I retreated to the Library on the floor below and closed the door, after giving orders to the servants to open all the windows pertaining to the upper floor to clear the air.

The next day, the smell having mostly worn off overnight, the men began their preliminary work by marking a grid on the walls which, Perriman explained, would later be used to align the pattern blocks. I confess that I was most disappointed at the end of the day that there was no colour on the walls as yet, but Perriman was most insistent that I would see a change upon the morrow. He is such an engaging fellow, that I was prepared to give him the benefit of the doubt.

I broke my fast early, so eager was I to see what progress had been made that morning. The method devised by Perriman proved more efficient than even he had imagined. One wall was already complete.

I watched enthralled as his men coated carved wooden blocks with dark pigment then pressed each one in turn against the paper on the wall. Each block fitted exactly into the grid the men had marked out the previous day. Every square had been given a number from one to six, and each block had the corresponding number carved on its back. Thus the men were able to print the pattern by using blocks numbered one to three on the bottom row then repeat the process on the row above with numbers four to six, all according to Perriman's master-plan which he made available to me.

Perriman explained that there were also half-blocks which would assist with the completion of the pattern in the corners of the room. Where the blocks could not fit, the pattern would be hand-drawn by himself. He assured me the dark colour of the pigment would fade as it dried on the plaster and, once his men had painted a colour wash over the entire room and over-painted the pattern, this initial outline would be entirely invisible. By the time supper was served, the outline on the walls was almost complete and I could begin to appreciate just how fine and rich the finished decoration would look.

And I was not disappointed! Perriman arranged for his men to work first on a small area of wall above the door. This way, he said, I could see how the painting would progress and if I was displeased with the colours, it should be but a small area to correct or replace. I watched as a wash of jade green was applied; not, as I had expected, using brushes, but by the application of clean cotton rags; his men dabbing the paint onto the wall so it showed darker in some places and paler in others.

Then the master painter, Mister Warren, took up his brushes and effortlessly produced an abundance of pink and white cherry blossom, while his two underlings painted the branches and bright green leaves. I was entranced by the ease and speed with which they worked together. Of course, I immediately gave Perriman permission to continue with the work.

So fascinated was I with the splendid scenes being revealed before my very eyes, that I desired a chair be placed in the middle of the room and would happily spend upwards of two hours or more each day gazing in admiration as the work progressed.

Did I mention that I had forbidden my dear wife to enter the room until it was complete? Each evening, at supper, she asked how the work was progressing hoping, I think, that I would let slip some morsel, but I was determined to keep her guessing, so the surprise would be the greater. When all was finally revealed, she wept with joy.

Each day brought new additions; exotic butterflies now occupied previously empty spaces amongst the foliage, and a veritable menagerie of tiny monkeys now scamper and play among the branches. White crested Ibis and other colourful birds, including fancy fowls, birds of prey and speckled doves, enrich the design beyond my expectations.

After many weeks, the design is complete and Perriman and his artisans have departed on their journey back to London, taking with them my Letters of Reference and a bag of golden guineas as reward for their endeavours on my behalf. I have already issued invitations to my neighbours to attend a dinner in one week's time, when I will reveal our new Chinese State Bedroom to them. Dorothy and I hope it will not be too long before you yourself feel able to leave Hardwick Hall and grace us with your presence at Erddig. Perhaps Margaret will accompany you? Dorothy would, I am sure, welcome her advice on the running of this much larger household.

Meanwhile, the furniture I ordered from London has arrived and the household is in a frenzy of activity with all the servants hard at work building and dressing the great bed, after which the other furnishings may be positioned. I am particularly proud of one noteworthy piece which has apparently languished in one of the rooms on the lower floor for many years.

Perhaps you may be able to enlighten me as to the circumstances under which our uncle acquired such a fine piece. I had always understood him to prefer plain pieces of furniture constructed with wood from our great English oaks.

This cabinet, in the *chinoiserie* style, consists in the lower half of four drawers surmounted by a *bureau*, above which sits a double fronted cupboard. The whole is lacquered in oxblood red, while delicate gold-leaf tracery outlines the many intricate scenes of ibis, pagodas, and fishermen. The interior of the cabinet is as highly decorated as the outer, with *oriental* mountain and river scenes aplenty; and tall vases adorn the inner facings of the doors. It will look very well when displayed in the room, I fancy.

Now the work is complete, and I gaze around in wonder, pleased that my 'vision' has come to fruition. It is truly the most beautiful room I have ever seen. To think that I, a humble countryman, should be in the auspicious position to enjoy such an exquisite work of art in my own house. I have truly been blessed by Dame Fortune.

May I extend our heartfelt good wishes to you and your family and implore you to consider our invitation to visit at your earliest convenience. As an added incentive perhaps, I would inform you that our late uncle's cellar still contains several bottles of a certain *Hock* which you are known to enjoy on occasion.

    Respectfully yours
        Simon Y------

                        Erddig Hall

15th November 1733

My dear old friend G-----,

What a time it has been since I was last in your company. Little did I know then that my circumstances were soon to change and my dear wife and I become elevated in society. You will, of course, remember my Uncle John Meller and his great kindnesses towards two starving undergraduates when he visited Oxford. How long ago those carefree days now seem, though scarcely seven years have passed.

You will recall from my previous letter that Dorothy and I planned to journey to North Wales for Christmas and the New Year. Upon our arrival, my uncle Meller at first appeared much the same as usual.

Though advanced in years, he retained a sturdy and upright figure, while his countenance bore testament to his continued enjoyment of the outdoors, it being his greatest pleasure to spend the daylight hours outside riding in the park and visiting the outlying farms of the Estate.

We noticed that my uncle seemed to tire easily and had developed a bothersome cough, which he attributed to the soaking he received about a week before our visit. Dorothy hastened to the kitchens and, with her own fair hands, devised a soothing drink of rum and hot water, seasoned with the juice of a lemon and sweetened with honey. Upon sipping a glass of the mixture, his cough subsided, and his usual good humour returned.

Dorothy gave instructions that a glass of the mixture should be brought to my uncle in his bedchamber each night, that his sleep may be untroubled by this ailment. She also curtailed his excursions into the countryside, inviting him to walk with her in the gardens instead, and to make notes of the improvements he planned, which he could easily do indoors as the gardens are overlooked from the great windows of the *Saloon* on the East aspect.

Unfortunately, his health deteriorated and he was confined to bed with a congestion of the chest, which no ministrations on the part of Dorothy or the local Doctor could disperse. As the bells rang out to welcome in the New Year, my uncle breathed his last. We buried him in the family mausoleum after a short service in the Chapel. The servants and estate workers were much distressed as he had been a good and kind master.

As he never married or had legitimate issue, I found myself his sole heir and, therefore, the new Squire. We returned home to our little cottage just long enough to pack up such belongings and furniture that we thought would be of use, and said our goodbyes to Dorothy's family and our neighbours, all of whom wished us well in our good fortune.

We returned to North Wales with mixed feelings; sorrow that my dear Uncle had been taken from us, conscious of the great legacy he had bestowed on me, and determined to make my mark. I have already embarked on a plan of restoration and improvements to the House.

If you have not already made arrangements, Dorothy has suggested, and I heartily concur, that you might wish to spend the Festive Season here with us. While we cannot hope to match the giddy round of festivities of London or our other great cities, there is much to be enjoyed in simple country pursuits at this time of year.

It is my most fervent hope that you will accept our invitation, and you shall have the honour of being the first person to occupy the new State Bedroom, which I have recently had furnished in the 'Chinese' style. Please advise your anticipated date of arrival by return.

   Yours in friendship
   Simon Y----

15th December, 1733

Dear G-----

Thank you for your letter, which arrived yesterday. Naturally, Dorothy is disappointed that our old friend will not be joining us for Christmas. Of course, I quite understand that my letter arrived after you had already accepted a prior invitation from no lesser a personage than the Duchess of M--------, though I did not realise you had been admitted into the intimate circle of such a notable member of society.

Our loss is her gain, as they say, and I am sure you will take much greater pleasure in her company than that of two 'country mice'. We will not be such a large gathering. Mourning is taken seriously by the good 'country folk' hereabouts. Though we are no longer required to wear black, we still choose to live simply and dress modestly. Dorothy has only ordered six new plain gowns for the Winter Season, while I find simple linen shirts, woollen hose, coats and knee breeches of a close-woven plain cloth more than adequate for my daily needs; though I may yet order my 'fripperies' to be brought out from storage. You remember, I am sure, my *penchant* for embroidered waistcoats?

Our guests are to include my parents-in-law, Mister and Mistress Hutton, and Mistress Hutton's mother Mistress Crowley, accompanied by Miss Maud Hutton, my wife's cousin. Our old neighbours, Major and Mistress Arthur Trent will also be with us for a few days *en route* to visit their family in Cheshire. Major Trent is to take up a commission overseas in the New Year. On Christmas Day itself we are to share our modest repast with the Reverend Palgrave, his wife and their daughter, Eularia, who is most accomplished, I believe, in the *feminine* arts of watercolour painting and needlepoint.

You must write immediately the celebrations are concluded, as I am sure Dorothy will be agog to hear of such grand adventures and excursions as you will no doubt experience in the environs of P----------- Castle.

Alas, I must close here. I am sure you appreciate that the business of running an estate is a constant drain on my time. There is so much to be done that I do not have a minute to call my own between ten in the morning and four in the afternoon. And, of course, there are the visits to our new neighbours, which Dorothy enjoys so much, which must be repaid by invitations to our own modest home.

    Yours sincerely
    Simon Y-----

10th January, 1734

Dear G----

Dorothy and I extend to you our sincerest commiserations in the matter of your unfortunate accident on Christmas Eve morn, and send our best wishes for a swift recovery from your injuries. How kind of the Duchess to allow you to recuperate at the Castle even though she and the rest of the party have gone abroad. I hope you are not too lonely there with only the servants at home. You must send me a line or two when you are restored to good health and returned to your rooms in Town.

Our own celebrations were beyond our modest expectations. The servants excelled themselves, decorating all the main rooms with greenery – ivy and suchlike – from the Park. Cook and the kitchen staff had laid in a good supply of game from the Estate and, for days before, sent out such tempting morsels for luncheon and supper that I became concerned our stocks would be exhausted before the great day arrived.

All our guests survived the long journey North without harm, the weather being dry and the roads firm. Though Mistress Crowley retired early to bed each evening, the remainder of the party stayed up until midnight. We men retired to the Library after dinner to play cards, joining the Ladies later for a musical interlude where we were indulged in a collection of country songs from Miss Maud Hutton, accompanied on the pianoforte by Mistress Trent.

After a service of thanksgiving in the Chapel on Christmas morning, Dorothy and I thanked the servants and estate workers and gave them a small gift each in appreciation of their hard work. Luncheon was served at one o'clock and there were many happy faces around our table that afternoon. Supper was a cold collation of pies and puddings while the servants ate their own Christmas feast. Much laughter and gaiety could be heard coming up the back stairs from their quarters and I had to ring the bell several times for the footman to come and build-up the fire in the *Saloon*.

The following morning, we awoke to find snow had fallen overnight to such a depth that it would be impossible for the Reverend Palgrave and his family to return to their own home, though it be but five miles from here. Major Trent set off on horseback along the drive towards the turnpike road, but returned almost at once, saying the way was impassable; though he believed a countryman with stout boots may find his way, the Major would not risk the horse.

We were confined indoors all that day finding

our amusements where we could. Mister Hutton undertook to begin a catalogue of my late uncle's books, of which there are several of the writings of the late author Defoe, as well as a number of bound Essays by Swift, in his own hand, though how my uncle came by them is not known to me. Mistress Crowley and Mistress Palgrave were content to sit close by the fireplace and speak of mutual friends.

Miss Maud Hutton expressed a desire to tour the house. Though I said that I was sure she has already seen most of it, she said she had not yet seen the Attics. I myself am unable to discern the fascination for poking about in the forgotten corners of other people's houses, but the Ladies seemed eager to explore, so there was nothing for it but to ring for the footmen to fetch several lanthorns containing fresh candles with which to light our way.

I confess that I had not previously set foot inside the attics, which extend the full length of the original house; the additional wings built by Uncle John shortly after its purchase in '09 are not linked in any way. My wife and her mother peered inside the room, but both declared they would not take one step further after observing the large cobwebs hanging from the rafters, and they retreated downstairs. Miss Maud Hutton and Miss Eularia Palgrave were made of sterner stuff and entered without hesitation; Mistress Trent elected to wait on the landing and a chair was fetched that she may rest more comfortably.

Major Trent, Reverend Palgrave and myself

contented ourselves with a slow perambulation along the centre of the room from one gable to the other and back again; a useful exercise as it revealed several areas of damage to the roof. I must speak to my Agent about effecting some repairs in due course.

Miss Maud and Miss Eularia made good use of their time and enjoyed themselves a great deal opening various trunks and boxes scattered about and declaiming passionately about their finds. Only through the exhortations of Mistress Trent were they prevented from dragging everything downstairs to be examined more thoroughly.

The next day, being Saint Stephen's Day and also Sunday, Reverend Palgrave presided over Morning Service in the Chapel. With our guests and servants all present for his sermon, he urged us to be thankful for the bountiful food and good companionship we had enjoyed over the previous days, and to pray to God that the snow would soon clear so he could attend to his duties around the Parish once again.

Fortuitously, his prayers were answered, and he and his family were able to return home the next day. Major and Mistress Trent left for Cheshire the day after, so we were just *en famille* for New Year's Eve.

All in all, I declare myself a lucky man to be in possession of a good wife, a fine house, and good friends to share it with me. Perhaps you also will one-day grace us with your presence in our humble

abode.
>Yours etcetera
>Simon Y----

Author's Note

These 'letters' from Simon Yorke are entirely fictional, though his cousin, Philip (later 1st Earl of Hardwick) is not.

A visit to Erddig in 2015, listening to the stories related by the room guides about the (very pink) Saloon and the highly decorated State Bedroom, led to many hours of research into the history of wallpaper and its increasing use as decoration in grand houses.

It is unlikely that the method of decoration I have described was used at Erddig. The actual date/year the State Bedroom was decorated has been changed to suit the story.

LOOK WHO'S COMING TO DINNER

By Fiona Knowles-Holland.

Guto looks to the sky for the weather.

"Fourteen percent chance of precipitation; humidity sixty-eight percent; pressure 1021 millibars," says one of the young fellows, looking at his phone.

Ay, I bet you're about right, Guto thinks voicelessly, looking at the ragged white clouds processing slowly across the blue sky. Clouds that seem to be looking down on the proceedings below with some curiosity. You're about right, lad. A few lazy wasps emerge into the sunshine.

It's the September sun he likes the best. Slow to banish the chill in the farmhouse. Adding sparkle to the dew drops in the grass for an hour or two after dawn. Fierce and bright come the afternoon, enough to enliven all living things for a festival of frenzy before thoughts turn to winter and hibernation. A *fiero* sun.

They have been lucky with the weather. Nobody could have predicted it would be so nice. Mind you, this crowd from up-London, if they could have ordered it, along with the canapes and champagne, they would have found a way.

"Come on, Pip." he calls his old sheepdog, in danger of tripping up one of the many bright young things mingling about, shouting into their mobile phones, to his side. Old boy's blind in one eye, mostly blind in the other and has cotton-wool for ears. "We'll just sit in the courtyard here and watch what's going on. She'll be out soon."

"Right you are, lass." he'd said when Megan had phoned him six months ago to say she was getting married.

"Thing is, I want to get married in Wales, in the village where Daddy grew up. It's kind of ... I dunno ... different. Alternative. Aren't you pleased, grandpa?"

"'Course."

Too bloody right, it's alternative, he'd grumbled when news broke out that his son had actually *bought* the chapel, ruined and derelict for decades, for thirty-thousand pounds. "You'd pay more than that for a fancy wedding at the Grosvenor Hotel these days," Matthew had told him, on one of his rare phone calls home. "In fact, anywhere within SW1 or SW2 is pricey." And, with a sigh, "What Megan wants, Megan gets. She's a bit Gothic. Likes to make a statement. At least we get something at the end of it." Guto silently raised an eyebrow at the end of the phone-line.

But the chapel! The last lights went out in the sixties. Old Eifion Lewis had a go at tacking some blue plastic sheeting over the vestry roof until he fell off. There's graffiti on the west wall. Pigeons fly in and out of the broken panes in the arched windows. Even the security grille on the door has been so challenged by the elements, it's fallen off its hinges. Inside, there's masonry dust and mice. Nobody wants to buy the place because you'd look out over your bespoke kitchen units, sipping coffee from one of those little coloured pods, at rows and rows of graves and the odd ancestry hunter popping up looking for old William ap Gryffyths and Dai Llewellyn ap Llewellyn and asking if, by the way, they could use your loo.

"I know, granddad, it's perfect!"

So, the villagers gamely volunteered their services to strim the grass, cut back the worst of the brambles, oil rusty hinges, and make their homes available for various members of the wedding party.

A gang of these bright young things had come up every weekend to strip out his barns for the wedding 'do', pulling down worm-eaten haylofts, making piles of metal scrap of the old rusty scythes, horse shoes, pitchforks, water pipes and bed springs, burning dusty hessian sacks, house-martin nests, windblown straw and baling twine, laughing like horses. He supposed it was alright. And then the girls came and put up bunting, trestle tables, fairy lights. It had been a bit of a surprise when twenty milk churns turned up in the back of a white van. "I've got some of those round the back of the shippen," he'd been about to tell the driver, but decided against it.

There's about a hundred people in the courtyard now, all milling around, mostly avoiding his eye. There's something very strange about the clothes they are wearing - but not as strange as the bride's. The crowd parts to allow Megan to walk towards him. She's wearing lace, black – to be expected, perhaps - webbing, open weave cut-off stockings, a crucifix, and elbow-length gloves – all black. Very little form or substance or, it has to be said, coverage. "You look lovely, my dear."

"Right, you stay here, granddad, and look after the children and make sure nobody eats the food. We'll be back in a couple of hours."

"Oh? Am I not ...?"

"No, granddad. Best you stay here. Come on, everyone, let's get married!"

Guto leans back against the sun-warmed stone blocks of the barn and watches as everyone trip traps over the cobbles and down the long lane towards the chapel on the other side of the road. A line of gloomy looking children stares at him, all with something of the Manson family about them.

"Right then, children, who's going to fetch me some of those cheesy pinwheels I saw going into the orchard a few moments ago?" They all run off except for a solemn looking lad. "What's your name?"

"Terence."

"Terence. I'm Guto. How do you do?" A wasp lands on Guto's outstretched hand and the lad flaps his hands and runs on the spot. "Hold still, Terence. No need to panic." Guto waits for the wasp to lift off into the air. "If you flap about, that makes them angry. When they're angry, they release this pheromone which sends the other wasps into a bit of a frenzy." Terence nods. "How old are you?"

"Fourteen."

"Well, Terence, since you're here, let me tell you about wasps. Fascinating creatures. Sit down next to me. Move along, Pip. That's right. Did you know that, if we didn't have wasps, we'd have no crops or vegetables? We'd be overrun by insects and aphids eating everything we want to eat. Worker wasps go out and get food for the growing larvae ..."

Terence is drawing circles in the dust with the point of his shoe.

"Did you know that wasps don't actual *eat* anything? They can't. Their waists are so tiny. So they chew the insects and aphids and feed the pulp to the larvae, and these larvae make this sort of sweet sticky spit which they feed back to the adults," Terence is looking dubious, "which is why wasps love our picnics and pop and ice-cream. Neat, eh?"

Terence's expression lifts slightly. "Where you from, then, Terence?"

"Shepherd's Bush."

"Oh, very nice. Where's that then?"

"London, of course."

"Doesn't sound very London." Terence smiles dimly. Guto wonders if he can summon up any more interesting insect facts. How about telling Terence how the queen makes one flight in Spring when she comes out of hibernation? During that flight, she must mate in order to lay her 300 fertilised eggs a day. But maybe the lad's a bit squeamish around the birds and the bees, or the birds and the wasps. So, Guto settles on, "How do you like Wales, then?"

Terence looks around at the old bricks reddening in the sunshine, the two pigeons on the telephone wire, glints in the stonework, the ewes fattening on the hillsides, the tightly wrapped silage, and shrugs. "Stupid place to have a wedding. Seems like a bad case of cultural appropriation if you ask me."

"Ah! Is that right?" Guto looks at the ground and ruffles Pip's ears. "Well, let's go and see where those cheesy pinwheels have got to, shall we?"

Guto rises slowly from the bench. No sign of the children but lines of caterers process, ant-like, between the kitchen and the orchard, carrying platters and trays, crockery and cutlery, bottles and ice-buckets.

He could have taken Terence to see a wasps' nest in the apex of the garden shed. Big as a football it is. Made out of pulp and saliva. Home to upwards of 8,000 wasps. Each born from a small, six-sided cell. Maybe later. He should probably find out what the other children are up to.

The wedding party returns. At least Megan looks happy. Hard to look 'radiant' perhaps in six-inch lace-ups.

She gives him a kiss as a harpist starts up with 'Men of Harlech.' Oh, for pity's sake! Maybe Terence was right.

There are three long tables each covered in food. Bitesize, colourful canapes. Butter pats floating in iced water. Breads. Cheeses, fruit jellies. Huge hams on the bone, the fat coating thick and succulent. Pork pies. Filo pastry parcels. Pickles. Chocolate coupes sweating slightly in the warmth.

Yet no-one approaches the tables. Over every item of food, yellow and black wasps, abdomens pulsing, membranous wings stretched backwards like the poles of downhill skiers, side-working jaws hacking off tasty morsels. Horrified guests stand and watch, dinner plates held close like shields.

Guto cannot help but smile at nature's own show of cultural appropriation.

NO MORE WORDS

(written for Nigel Johnson, set in the Hope Community Library)
By Susanne Allcroft

My work here is nearly done. A day of people visiting, looking at the books, flicking through the pages, searching out favourite authors and booking out their reading materials for the weeks ahead. Youngsters with their parents look for the latest children's books in excitement. It's great to see, the opening of young minds to endless thoughts, concepts, possibilities and dreams – the next generation of book worms. A gentleman sits in the corner reading. I say gentleman because those qualities radiate from within him – courteous and polite, respectful of fellow bibliophiles, quiet, gentle and intelligent. He reads with interest, slowly turning the pages and adjusting his glasses now and then. Absorbed by each word on the page, he sometimes has a wry smile when something appeals to his sense of humour. Come to think of it, he's been here all day… all week even. On reflection, he's always been here. I'm locking up the library, dimming the lights as the daylight outside ebbs. I turn to the gentleman in the corner to ask him to leave but he's gone already, faded quietly into the bookshelves, he is forever lost amongst the pages.

OBSERVATION: A SLICE OF FARM LIFE

By Fiona Knowles-Holland

I live in a house of many windows but, curiously, they all face either north or south. If looking one way, it is into shadow for most of the year, except in midsummer, when the sun sits on the apex of the roof and creates only narrow pavements of shade. Look the other way and – if I weren't such a slattern at cleaning my windows – you might look into year-round southerly warmth and light.

For some reason, only one window faces either east or west. From no window can you watch the sun rising and only one very small bathroom window, set high in a towering gable, allows you to look west at the night's left-over moon.

The house is set on an agricultural axis. The dairy, the apple store, the butchery, the summer kitchen all face north, allowing only cool air to blow a bloom across the apples or to riffle the surface of the warm milk.

I imagine the original builder liked his blaze of glory, welcoming his guests from the road in front of the house up the stone bright steps. They would step onto the petals of sunlight from the fanlight above the heavy, sun-warmed door.

I wish I could look through a window and see the farm as it was. So much to see. Drovers ululating their cattle from Llandegla, splashing through the black brook on their way to the Midlands. The Liverpool owner's land agent calling for the quarterly rent. Early motor cars. The last few seconds of life of two motorcyclists. One careless, one just in the wrong place at the very wrong time. A dogfight over Buckley. Funeral processions up the hill; wakes coming down the hill. Horses over the cobbles. Welsh mountain sheep brought down to their winter pastures – unmannerly, rough as gypsies, no respecters of hedges or field boundaries, tearing rag-tag through the hedgerows, bringing their mob ways with them.

Thin times. Fat times.

Wind through broken slats-times. Sweet cows' breath rising from the byre–times. Wisps of three-year old sour hay–times. Wooden lofts groaning with plenty–times. Generations born, schooled, destined, sweated, feted, till propped and plumped by the fire, then mourned.

How I wish I could look through a window in time and meet those who loved the farm as I do. Maybe their souls hang like dockets in the ancient yew on the roadside, as will mine.

SLEEPING DRAGONS

By S W Fellows

Protected by mountains and sea
Wales is very dear to me.
What beautiful stories can be told?
Or are they only for the old?

Its own language has been oppressed
Because its conquerors knew best.
So, the nation speaks half and half
And its language is viewed with a laugh.

Castles draw tourists, keen to see
The ancients' forms of tyranny.
Slate museums with wares to sell
But slate production was a living hell.

Coal was no better,
Everything was black.
Hauling baths of water
Young women would crack.

Coughing and coughing

Becoming diseased
Quarry men and miners
Were not appeased.

Closing the pits
Did them a favour
But regarding new jobs
Bosses managed to waiver.

No bread on the table
No money in the pot
No pony in the stable
The unemployed lot.

But over time
Hope raised its head
And alternative methods
Meant the family were fed.

So now the ancient dragon is curled up tight
A fragment of its once wondrous might.
At sporting events you'll hear it roar
From hilltop high to the seashore.

So, this is Wales,
And my nationality.
My retreat, my home
My own country.

THE DINNER LADY OF YSGOL NEWYDD

By Catherine Jones

"Stop *shaking that ketchup machine, you naughty girl!*" screamed Old Mrs Jones the dinner lady. She waved her spatula at me as I pounded on the top of the sauce machine. Her glabellar complex forced itself into a canyon-like crevice in the middle of her eyebrows, but I carried on until some sauce came out. Sadly, my short-lived joy was merely ephemeral as the sauce sprayed across my chest and over my light blue school blouse.

"*I told you to stop it! Now look what you've done!*" she screeched. The more she screeched, the higher pitched and more prominent her Wrexham accent became.

"*Ya Mam's gonna kill you now! I don't have to!*" she spat, with glee-filled eyes as she turned and marched back into the canteen.

I looked down at my shirt. Oh no, it was

filthy, Mam would have to wash me another one. But even more disappointingly, I still had no sauce on my hot dog! I would not be able to stomach the cardboard textured bread with the limp, generally unwell looking sausage placed on top of it unless I had some tomato sauce. As her back turned, I made a last-ditch attempt to hammer the top of the sauce dispenser. This time, a large blob of the overly sugary, bright red and presumably now barred 1980s red sauce slid perfectly across the top of my hotdog. Hearing the rattle, Mrs Jones spun round.

"See?" I retorted cheerfully, "I've mended it for ya now!"

Mrs Jones huffed.

"Now leave it alone!" She glared and dug her spatula deep down into the slop as she began to serve the remaining unfortunate children their school dinners. She stood proudly behind the trays of luminous green peas, the sweetcorn that looked as if it had recently been harvested from the field next to Sellafield, and the hotdogs and chips which looked as if someone had made them out of plastic for a cruel joke. It was enough to save dentists all over North Wales thousands of trips from children needing their teeth removed once they had bitten into one of Mrs Jones' hotdogs. If that did not crack your teeth, the potent, sugar-laden sauce would surely disintegrate them.

Mrs Jones was the most feared dinner lady of them all. Five feet tall, she towered above you. Her long, dark blue pinafore came to rest on her knees just above where her wrinkly stockings ended, held up precariously by balancing on her varicose veins. Her face was hot and as red as the most fierce Welsh Dragon and her eyes glared into your very soul if you bravely whispered a quiet *"No thanks"* as she offered you her home made semolina. A refusal of this meant that you would be forced to eat her rice pudding instead; a fate worse than death.

After the dinner bell rang, any kid still left trying to chomp their way through one of her burgers or sausages, made with the finest toenails, lips and animal nether regions, was made to forfeit their next break. If they dared to throw their dinner away or failed to eat every scrap they would be made to help empty the bins and clear the whole hall.

"Awww," I cried to Mum as she picked me up from the school gate.

"Whatever's the matter?" she asked, aghast to see me in such distress.

"Y, you, didn't pack me any sandwiches!" I sobbed.

Mum stopped walking immediately. My little sister, sleeping in the pushchair, woke up and began to cry as Mum stopped so forcefully that she jolted her whole body.

"Oh." said Mum quietly. "Sorry, did you have to eat....school dinners?"

"Yeees!" I wailed loudly.

"Oh love," she sympathised. "I'm sorry."

"Oh Mam," I said, swiftly stopping crying, "I got sauce on my blue shirt."

Mum's face dropped as she looked at my shirt.

"What on earth were you doin'?" she asked.

"Well, you didn't pack my sandwiches..." I reiterated. "So I 'ad to 'ave school dinners! And they're horrible, so I needed sauce on it, and I pressed the sauce machine too 'ard! Then it broke and..."

"Bloomin' 'eck!" replied Mum, "I'm sure when I see her, she'll tell me all about it!"

I nodded my head.

"Yeah, I remember her dinners when I was a kid." replied Mum. "They tasted bloomin' awful then! To be honest, I dunno how I'm still 'ere, havin' to eat them myself."

I skipped home along the pavement. The sun shone brightly. Mum promised to make me some Birdseye crispy pancakes and chips for tea as long as I ate my salad. Mum's food was nice, I liked salad, so I was happy.

At teatime, I sat down to my tea and tucked into the pancakes. I took the jar of salad cream and smothered it all over my salad. All of a sudden, a voice shrieked from behind me.

"Stop hitting that bottle so hard, you don't need that much sauce you naughty girl!"

Oh no, not her again! I'd had enough of her for one day. Glumly, I put the bottle down.

"Don't need it anyway!" I huffed. "Anyway, nothin' tastes as bad as your dinners in school."

She raised her hand and went to slap me across the head.

"*You cheeky little rat!*" she screeched. I ducked

out of the way laughing. God she was annoying and very, very embarrassing at times but fair do's she was ace. Especially when sometimes she got me out of scrapes and sent the school bullies packing when it was my turn to be picked on.

"Now, now, stop it!" said Mum as she dried the pots by the sink. "She's right, your dinners are horrible mother!" she retorted as she pointed her finger to me. "And you, don't be so cheeky to your Nan!"

THE HARE AND THE ECLIPSE.

By Susanne Allcroft

The hare awakened suddenly one sharp January night. The air was still and quiet and magical. A glittering frost formed silently on leaves and in the elbows of knotty branches and on wilted flowers patiently hanging their heads, waiting for spring. A tangible cloud of fog had drifted into the distance leaving clarity lit by a large bright moon that cast chilling silver shadows across the landscape.

It felt like the perfect time for a bewitching reacquaintance with the countryside beyond his winter retreat.

The movement of his eyes opening, and his nose twitching created no sound, but the stretching of the hare's neck and his powerful hind legs caused an audible shiver in the dried grasses of his nest. He moved out to the centre of the field, his silhouette illuminated by the moonlight, shyly took a glance both ways and then stood, an impressively tall and lean figure. His ears prominent and alert, listening for any sign of trouble, he tilted his head towards the sky and studied it curiously. He felt a spiritual calibration as he considered the position of the moon. The alignment was beginning, the moon gliding slowly into the earth's shadow, the circle becoming obscured and ragged, the lustrous glow fading. The hare felt a tremor of excitement and raised both front paws. Still nothing moved, the silence was uncanny, none of the usual nocturnal sounds of owls calling, field mice rustling or the harsh bark of a fox.

Then came the awe-inspiring colours, the ruby and orange glow of the light refracting from the sun onto the moon. Large and glowing with a bittersweet blush of red, this wolf moon did not signify an ending but rather an exciting new beginning. Where the suns curved rays could not reach, lay rugged, dark patches that, to eyes from earth, took on images of faces and expressions on the moon's surface.

The hare looked across at the gentle rise and open space sweeping ahead of him, inviting him to run boundlessly using all the kinetic energy stored in his hind legs. In the seconds of partial darkness, he appeared to hover above the ground, a fleeting figure zig zagging over the frozen earth before he aligned himself with the cosmos. Swathes of silver cloud criss-crossed the sky, as if charting his journey, an eerie moonshine reappeared capturing a flash of his black and white scut as it flagged his pilgrimage into the new year. Then, just as a shooting star blazed an arch across the brightened sky and dropped out of sight, the hare too was gone, evaporating into the night before dawn could capture him. He left only his own form depressed into the flattened grasses where he had been sleeping, for somebody to imagine his existence.

Written following the sighting of a hare in the fields of North Wales on the eve of a lunar eclipse.

TIME TO GO.
By Susanne Allcroft

Alex was a gentle, studious boy. He loved nature, and the forested hills to the south of Edinburgh were his home throughout the summer months before the weather turned cold. At 15, he had plans to study Marine Biology at University and spent hours collecting crustaceans and seagrasses from the coastal areas near his house. When the war started in 1939, he looked up at the roaring planes heading to the Firth of Forth seeing them merely as a noisy distraction in his otherwise peaceful life. Three years later, when the noise had failed to abate, Alex found himself conscripted to the RAF, all plans of academia temporarily squashed.

In January 1943, his squadron started to undertake training flights over the Welsh hills from Tilstock Airfield in Shropshire. The familiarity of the landscape reminded him of home, the endless rolling hills covered in frosted pines far from the main bombing routes of the German aircraft.

8pm, January 11th, 1943; "Time to go", Alex and his seven colleagues rose from a bench in the draughty hangar, stamping their feet and rubbing their gloved hands together against the cold. The Armstrong Whitworth Whitley bomber waited on the frozen airstrip; flurries of sleet captured in the lights. A sideways glance between Alex and the youngest of the airmen, David, aged 18, revealed the tension that the young men felt as their maiden flight was about to begin. At 28, the eldest two airmen, Robert from Middlesex and William from Alberta, Canada had plenty of experience and walked with confidence towards the bomber, adjusting the straps on their headgear and checking their watches. Alex fumbled with his seat belt, unsure if he had strapped himself in properly.

Some 25 miles to the west, the lofty village of Bwlchgwyn lay under a thick blanket of snow. Not unusually for this time of year, the villagers were checking on elderly residents, bringing food and logs to those who were housebound. Rhys, a gentle and studious boy, stared into the fire, mesmerised by the glowing embers and low flickering flames. "Time to go" his father said, and Rhys pulled on his hat and gloves to make the short walk home through the snow.

Rhys loved the outdoors and spent clear nights in Bwlchgwyn studying the stars. He thought himself lucky to live in a place where the skies were so vast and impressive. The blackouts during the war had given him even more opportunity to stargaze, seeking out celestial bodies and galaxies, silver dust against the blackness. Tonight, though, the sky was full of snow clouds obscuring his view.

Rhys and his father paused on the sharp bend by the Great War memorial and looked towards Moel Famau, aware of the sound of a low engine sputtering nearby.

Alex wished he could see the mountains of Moel Famau and Moel Arthur below. He imagined what it might feel like to scale the tracks and paths to the top then take in the boundless view but was increasingly more mindful of the dull pain which had started in the pit of his stomach when the plane took off. The noise of the engine faltering and the sudden dips towards the mountainside made him wonder if this was what an aircraft in trouble felt like. He tried to study the expressions of his colleagues, but their headgear obscured the panic on their faces.

When Rhys looked skyward, the stars that he usually identified as planets and constellations seemed fiery and agitated, tumbling towards the frozen ground. The floundering plane descended in front of his eyes, a burst of bright flames against the jet-black night. The snow appeared amber and swirled above the wreckage, father and son could only watch in horror.

At home, the telephone was ringing. A call for the local policeman who lodged with the family, an incident to investigate just outside the village. On his night off, the policeman was enjoying a warming brandy in the local hostelry when Rhys' father arrived to collect him.

Navigating the icy roads, they drove the car across the moors to the crash site. Born and bred in Bwlchgwyn, they knew every twist and turn that would lead them to Rhydtalog where the plane lay.

Alex's seatbelt, unfastened throughout the flight, opened as the plane hit the ground, flinging him out onto the snow and away from the burning wreckage. Badly injured, his mind raced through the events of the evening. His thoughts tumbled onto the ambitions he had yet to achieve, the conversations he wanted to have with friends and family, the places he had wanted to visit and explore. Paralysed by his injuries, he lay back into the snow and closed his eyes.

Seven airmen were dead on impact. The eighth, a gentle and studious young man with a passion for nature, still drew laboured breaths. The men of Bwlchgwyn put Alex in the car and drove him towards the hospital. His last breath was taken in the Gegin woods, on the outskirts of the village, his last memory the warmth and comfort of the men that tried to save him, who spoke to him of home and his family in Scotland. Rhys's father stared at the pale, lifeless arm that extended from the torn, scorched fabric, young skin barely exposed to the traumas of life. He noticed the watch on Alex's wrist; his life ended, the hands of the watch continued to move, keeping beat around the watch face when his heart no longer could, a dynamic marking of time after Alex's short lifespan had ended. He felt a deep sadness at the paradox and often thought of it over the years when telling the story to his children and their families.

2019.

Rhys and his son sit on a bench on a warm summer evening. The sun is dipping behind Moel Famau, painting the sky with splendid colours. Rosy clouds hang above the ridgeline and a warm breeze lightly touches the grasses and wildflowers that stretch between the bench and the mountain. The only sounds are the sheep and cows grazing peacefully in the valley below. Rhys's son is a gentle, studious boy, he loves nature and often walks amongst the pineclad hills of Bwlchgwyn in search of wildlife. He hopes to go to University one day, maybe become a botanist, but for now, he is content to take in the view of Rhydtalog from the bench erected in memory of Alex and his comrades, and enjoy the post war peace and tranquillity.

Inspired by a true story but with fictional elements. Bwlchgwyn village has marked the plane crash with a bench that looks to the place where it happened.

TWM GOLAU

By Peter Jones

Holding my hand as we walked down the lane, he looked up at me and said, 'Did you walk down here when you were a boy, Taid?'

'I did, Dewi bach. But it was all so different then. It was called Station Lane, well, it still is. It was much busier with people going back and forth, it was noisy and steamy, with people and dogs, and porters and postmen. Oh it was very different. Even the streetlights were different.'

'The streetlights? How?'

'Well, Dewi, they were gas in those days. And there was a man who used to come along at dusk and switch them all on, then at dawn, switch them all off again. He lived in one of those houses at the end of the lane, number three Railway Terrace. Twm Golau we kids called him, Tom the Light for those who didn't have the Welsh.'

'What? A switch like a light switch? Like in the house? Why did it need anyone to do that?'

'No, bach,' I chuckled, 'each light had to be switched on so the gas could come through. He had a long stick with a hook on it. He'd pull a lever down to let the gas out and push it back up to close it off. Of course, when we thought no-one was looking, we'd jump up and switch them on. We'd come down here, you see, to catch the train to Aberddu to go to the beach. We'd switch the lights on and run down the lane for the train, Twm Golau's dog, Clwt, chasing and barking and running through our legs. He thought it was a game, too. Then off we'd go on the train. They had compartments then, six seats in each one, but we'd all pile in. There were the twins, June and Jennifer, me and my brother, your great Uncle Llew that is, and your Aunty Enid, my little sister, and Ifan Fferm, Joe, who was evacuated from England during the war, and never went back, and Llinos, your Nain, whose house Joe lived in.

'When we get back, I'll show you a picture, your Nain will have kept it safe. Oh, we thought the summers would never end, then.' I sighed deeply at this nostalgic moment.

We walked in silence as we passed Railway Terrace and I pointed my stick at number three, Dewi nodded and I fancied I saw a curtain twitch. I opened the gate onto the old station. Just a platform and a fence on this side, with all evidence of that post-war bustle of my childhood gone.

Looking carefully, I could just about see, in my mind's eye, the stand for the milk churns, the office where the letters and parcels were sorted, the ticket office, and I tried to remember where the machine was where we could weigh ourselves for a penny. I looked across to platform two which was just as bare. The platform where we would wait in expectation for the train to take us to the beach. Shouting and laughing, running up and down, over the bridge to this platform and back, playing tick and, no doubt, humbugging the grown-ups. *Happy days*, I thought, *happy days*.

I turned to the end of the platform and saw that the bridge was still there, but there was no longer any need for it as the lines had been pulled up in the 1960s and now it was all grass and meadow flowers. But, for old time's sake, I'd take Dewi over the bridge.

'Well, Dewi bach, let's see you run over the bridge to the other platform. Go on boy, I'll be right behind you.'

Dewi ran ahead, but, as I got to the middle of the bridge and looked down at where the track would have gone into the distance, I thought I saw a wisp of white smoke and I almost heard the whistle of a train. *Day dreaming, Pedr, you old fool*, I said to myself, but I felt a shiver before I moved on.

'Tud yma, Taid!'

Dewi had all the patience of a small lad, and I had the agility of a septuagenarian. My knees creaked as I descended to the platform and looked at what used to be a small coal yard beyond, with its broken fences, rusting hopper and dilapidated buildings. Trees and weeds were growing through the cracked tarmac. *What happened to Gwilym Glo?* I thought to myself. *Must be dead by now. Just like Twm*

Golau.

I saw an old upturned tea chest and wondered if it would take my weight. I decided to risk it and, putting my weight on my stick, I gingerly sat down and watched my grandson scampering about the platform and yard. It was an adventure playground from yesteryear. As he disappeared behind a broken wall, I shouted for him to be careful. 'I'm alright, Taid, don't fuss.' It is true, boys will be boys. I took in the mid-afternoon summer sun, closed my eyes for a moment and my mind drifted to those days that seemed so carefree. I could hear the whistle of a train, the hiss of steam and, I swear, the bark of a dog.

'Here Clwt,' so named because of the white patch over its left eye. Like all border collies, he was fast and supple and ran circles round us when we were kids. 'Here Clwt,' again that voice. Was I dreaming or was it real? The voice seemed vaguely familiar, from my childhood, it was ... it was ... I couldn't remember.

'Taid, Taid. Wake up.' Dewi pulled at my sleeve and I opened my eyes, slowly.

'What is it?' I said.

'Did you see them? Did you see the dog and the old man?'

'What dog, what man?'

'Over there,' he said, pointing beyond platform one, at the lane that we'd come down not so long ago. 'He was calling the dog. It was a sheepdog with a white patch over one eye.

I was now completely out of my reverie and paying close attention to Dewi. 'Where?'

'Going up the lane and stopping at every light. He seemed to be reaching up with a stick and the dog was running up and down. But they've gone now, Taid. Where have they gone?'

Twm Golau? Surely not. To my young eyes he was old in the 1950s. Now, in the twenty first Century he'd be a hundred and twenty or thirty. No, the boy's imagination had been fired by my story and the new playground he'd been introduced to, surely.

I shook my head and the past fell away. 'Time for tea, Dewi.' He dashed back over the bridge and I followed. Again, I stopped halfway, but could see or hear nothing. *Imagination, Pedr*, I thought, *imagination, it's a powerful thing.*

As we walked back up the lane Dewi continued to ask questions about who lived in Railway Terrace when I was a boy, what the trains were like, how many people worked at the station, and more. My childhood memories seemed to fascinate him. He was particularly interested in Twm Golau and Clwt. Back at the house, he told his Nain all about it and she showed him the old photos, pointing out the various people that I'd told him about.

***

The summer was gone, now, and Dewi was back with his Mam and Dad. It was autumn, and I'd taken to having an evening stroll after supper. "After dinner, rest a while. After supper walk a mile." I could hear my Taid telling me so many years ago.

I don't know why, but I decided to walk to the old station. It was still light, but it would be getting dark soon.

As I neared the end of Station Lane, I thought I saw the curtains twitch in number three. *Just like last summer*, I thought. Crossing the bridge, I smiled at the memory of Dewi running about and enjoying himself whilst I reminisced. A gust of wind suddenly brought an autumn chill, I shivered and turned back. I jumped as I thought I heard a door slam. *The wind*, I thought.

As I turned away from Railway Terrace and looked up the lane, I noticed the streetlights coming on and I quickened my pace.

As the shadows grew and dusk descended, I saw a man further up the lane, walking towards me. He had a long stick in one hand and a dog ran about his feet. It was strange, but as he passed each light, no shadows were cast, not his nor the dog's.

We were very close to each other, now, and he looked at me and said "Nos da, Pedr bach, nos da." And then he walked on. I turned and saw him and the dog fading as they walked into the ever-darkening evening. At the end of the lane, I fancied I saw the glow of a coal fire as one of the doors opened, then a small bang as it shut again.

'Twm Golau and Clwt the dog? Surely not.' I said, aloud, to myself. I hurried home and told Llinos my story.

'Imagination is a powerful thing, Pedr. A powerful thing, indeed,' she said.

UPS AND DOWNS

By David Powell

Hills and valleys, sheep high on mountains
breathing sweet fresh air,
Men and boys in deep dark pits, just
dust and gas for them,
Sheep on mountains, lush grass to
eat just there at their feet
Men in the dark, sandwiches with blackened
crust, hands thick with dust,
At day's end up into the light for
the long walk home,
Tired and dirty to the hot tin bath,
fireplace full of coal
From that horrid place, the face.

WALES ACROSTIC POEM

By Susanne Allcroft

Wales
A land
Lost in song
Ever reaching hills and falls
Sink into sheep-clad valley walls

Y DDRAIG GOCH

(The Red Dragon)
By Julie Huxley

This story begins long ago in the time of myth and legend, when the Celtic King, Vortigen, seeks to escape the marauding Saxons. Fleeing into Wales, the King chooses the site now known as Dinas Emrys to build his castle, but this proves much harder than anyone could have foreseen...

A week after Vortigen's men had started work, the chief mason requested an audience.

'I am sorry, Sire, but I fear we will have to find another place to build.' Idwal stood before the King, twisting his hat in his hands.

Vortigen scowled. 'There is no better place,' he said.

'You are right, Sire, but we build strong walls each day, leave each night satisfied with our work, only to return to find a ruin.'

'Dig deeper,' Vortigen said. 'This is the only place for my castle. I will have no other.'

Idwal bowed and returned to his men who toiled for five more days, returning to fallen castle walls each morning. On the sixth night they decided to sit and watch to witness the destruction for themselves.

'What do you think is happening?' Cledwyn asked, cupping his hands round a bowl of hot stew, warming them against the clammy chill of the rising mist.

Idwal shook his head. 'It is a strange thing indeed. The King may need the counsel of his sorcerers; I have never known such a mystery as this.'

'Farmer Trefor told me that since we've been trying to build the castle, his crops have started to fail, and he found his best cow dead in the barn.'

'I heard that Gwendolyn's young husband took a sudden fever on the first night the walls fell,' Idwal said. 'A strong, strapping lad he was, dead before sunrise.'

As he spoke, an eerie howl sounded, and the ground moved below them. He started to his feet, eyes dark in the firelight. A high-pitched scream followed, and the walls began to sink. Holes opened, swallowing the fire and the men's tools.

Scrambling for purchase, they fled to lower ground as the unearthly moans and cries rose and fell, reducing the strong walls to dust. They didn't stop running until they reached the King's camp.

By first light the next day the royal sorcerers were sent far and wide to find a child for blood sacrifice.

'He must be the result of a union between a human mother and a father from the Other World.'

they said.

'It is the only way to appease the evil spirits who have cursed our people and withered our land.'

***

Three men sat next to the fire in The Trout Inn, arguing over their neighbour, Dylan and the strange vision one of them claimed to have witnessed.

'He's right, the father's not normal. I saw a sleek grey seal in the lake, playing and eating with its fellows. After a bit, the others swam away and this one popped its head up and looked around. It came out of the water, there was a shimmer and Dylan rose up, naked as a babe on its birthday.'

Owain shook his head. 'Don't be ridiculous, Eynon. You drink so much of that moonshine of yours, it's pickled your brains. I saw you once, fighting your own shadow, screaming that the Black Dog was chasing you.'

'What about Myrddin?' Deykin asked. 'They took him to the lake to be baptised and the moment his toes touched the water he swam away with the fishes, leaving his poor mother weeping on the shore.'

'Says who?' Owain swung his tankard in their direction, slopping ale on the table. 'You're a pair of old gossips.'

'I would hear more of this Myrddin.'

A deep voice made them jump. A hooded figure stood before them, his rich sable cloak sweeping the floor.

The men blinked through their befuddled vision trying to discern their visitor's features but they remained invisible, although Deykin caught a mirror-eyed reflection in the firelight.

'Tell me about this boy,' the stranger commanded and they found they could not refuse him.

'He's just one of the local children.' Owain said. 'My companions have had too much ale. It is all gossip and fairy tale.'

The stranger directed his unnerving gaze at Deykin, who shrank into his woollen coat under the chilling glare.

'You said he swam away at his baptism. Is he then a pagan child?'

'N-no, sir. He is properly baptised. Tis just a jest, as he has always been able to swim like a fish.'

The sable cloak swirled and the stranger vanished, leaving the men blinking in confusion, each staring at his companion. Eynon spoke first: 'More ale?'

'Yes, yes. More ale!'

The rest of the evening passed in merry song, all memory of the cloaked man erased.

Many miles away the stranger was conferring with his fellows. 'The child is named Myrddin. We have found our blood sacrifice.'

Sitting in their tidy little cottage in Carmarthen, Myrddin and his mother, Rhianna, looked into the scrying stone and waited.

The knock came at dawn. Rhianna stood in

the doorway, arms crossed, head held high. She surveyed her visitors with narrowed eyes. A long, lean figure swathed in a rich black cloak stood at the door, flanked by burly men in scarlet tunics, hands ready on their swords.

'I am Kedivor, sorcerer and counsellor to the King. There is a curse upon this land. We need a sacrifice, a child born of an earthly mother and a father from another world. Your son, Myrddin is the one we seek.'

'I have no such child. His father is of this earth, just as we are.'

'I think you lie, Madam. We know your husband, Dylan, changes into a seal when he takes to the water and spends time at sea communing with the creatures there.'

Rhianna barked with laughter. 'You are taken in by rumour and superstition. My husband is a strong swimmer and a successful fisherman. These wild claims start in jealous mouths.'

Kedivor raised his hand. He stared into Rhianna's eyes and she could not look aside from their mesmerising pull.

'We have come for Myrddin.' he said. 'The King commands it.'

'The King has no right to my son. Crops fail. Folk and animals die every year. I will not give him up.'

The soldiers drew their swords and she nodded towards them.

'Such a fearless King who would murder an innocent child to prove his fortitude and strength instead of building elsewhere!'

'Mother.'

Rhianna spun on her heel. Myrddin stood at her elbow.

'I will go.'

'A wise choice.' Kedivor said, looking at Rhianna. 'You will be handsomely compensated for your son's wisdom.'

Stepping forward, he took Myrddin's arm and with a swirl of his cloak, he and his men, were gone.

Myrddin blinked, looking around as his feet touched the ground. Seconds ago, he had been standing at his mother's side; now, he stood in an opulent tent – large enough to hold fifty men. Banners and tapestries hung around the sides and fur skins were spread thickly over the earthen floor.

A stocky man stood before him, red hair and beard stark against his skin.

'So, Kedivor, this is our saviour?' He inspected Myrddin as he would a horse. 'Hmm. Seems like a normal boy to me. I sense no witchery around him. Where is your proof of his otherworldly parentage?'

Kedivor bowed low. 'Your Majesty is wise. This boy's ordinariness is a disguise that hides his true nature. The father is a shape-shifter and his child swam away in fear at his baptism.'

'Well, boy,' Vortigen said. 'what say you?'

Myrddin stood tall and faced the King. 'I could not say, sire. I was just a babe.'

Vortigen's eyebrows vanished into his hair

and his lips twisted.

Myrddin felt his belly clench in fear as Kedivor grabbed him by the scruff of the neck and shook him. 'Show your King some respect.'

'Please sire – I meant no...' Myrddin gasped, raising his eyes, but Vortigen was laughing.

'Let him go, Kedivor. He speaks the truth, does he not?'

Kedivor opened his hand and Myrddin fell to his knees.

Vortigen sat before him and rubbed his beard. 'Well, Myrddin, we have a problem. I need a strong castle to protect my people against the Saxons, yet the Gods seem set against me.'

Myrddin looked into the King's weary face. 'It is not the Gods, sire. It is feuding dragons.'

Kedivor flushed and stepped forward. 'What fabrication is this? You lie to save your skin.'

Vortigen held up his hand. 'I would have proof. Are you not sick of bloodshed?'

He turned his eyes back to Myrddin, who reached into his tunic and pulled out the scrying stone. Passing his hand over it, the smooth blue stone turned as clear as glass.

Looking into its depths, Myrddin could see two sleeping dragons, one white and one red, by a lake underneath the mountain.

He handed the stone to Vortigen. 'They sleep now, sire, but as the men work through the day, the dragons wake and the red, trapped below by the white, battles the invader through the night, hence the loss of your castle walls by morning.'

Vortigen stared into the stone for a long moment. 'Send for my men, Kedivor. We need to start digging.'

The men dug around the clock for three days. Myrddin watched in both anticipation and fear. The stone had never let him down, but he knew his life was forfeit if he failed.

Lost in thought a sudden shout jolted him into the present.

A huge bloodied head reared out of the earth, as a white dragon hauled itself upwards, spurting flame and scattering the men. Emerging close behind, a red dragon sank his claws into the white's tail, clambering over it onto solid ground. Turning with a snarl, the white faced its foe, striking across the red's flank.

Rearing back, the red opened his jaws. Brilliant flame shot forth blinding the watching crowd.

Myrddin blinked against the brightness but Vortigen did not move. His hands clenched; sometimes one strayed to his sword as if he longed to join the battle.

Lifting into the air, the red knocked the white onto its side; the crowd cheered as it ripped at the soft underbelly, but the white was quicker. Whipping his head round he sunk his teeth deep into the red dragon's neck. Crimson gouts spurted forth, creating a gory wallow as the combatants fought to the death.

Myrddin gagged on the metallic stench as he

watched the red begin to stagger, his eyes darkening. The white roared, striking a final blow as his rival dropped to the ground.

The red dragon lay like stone, eyes closed tight.

Silence fell, broken only by the flap of cloaks in the bitter wind. Bowing his head, Myrddin felt the sting of his hair as it whipped across his face.

Beside him, Vortigen drew his sword. The crowd fled, leaving Vortigen and Myrddin standing alone.

Vortigen gripped his sword with both hands. 'Vile beast! This land is mine. I will fight to keep it.'

Black eyes blazing, the dragon reared, but as he did so, Myrddin felt a tremor below his feet.

The red dragon had begun to rumble. It grew to a boom, shaking the earth with its power. The partly excavated hole gaped wide and swallowed them.

Myrddin and Vortigen clung to the edge, watching as the red flapped and twisted, sinking his talons into the wing of the white, ripping through membrane and tendons.

Screaming with rage, the white plummeted to the bottom of the hillside, a landslide of rocks and earth burying it once again.

Seconds later the Red Dragon burst into the air, turning and swooping low over Vortigen and Myrddin. His blood, sticky and warm against their skin, felt like an anointment.

ABOUT HOPE WRITING GROUP

Welcome to the Hope Community Library Creative Writing Group's first Anthology, *Wales*. We hope you enjoy reading work produced by members of the group since our launch in March 2018. Our genres range from poetry, science-fiction, contemporary fiction and magical realism, to flash and crime. The only thing we can't come up with is a snappier title for our group!

BIOGRAPHIES FOR ANTHOLOGY

Susanne Allcroft

A novice writer from a teaching background, the creative writing club has rekindled Susanne's love of writing and the English language. She has learnt so much from spending time with accomplished writers and hopes to develop more skills to enhance her written work. She is a qualified proofreader and editor and lives in a beautiful, inspiring part of North Wales.

Margaret Arndt

Margaret's inspiration in poetry is mainly focussed on people closest to her together with nature and its surroundings.

Phil Burrows

Phil has an imagination that runs faster than his ability to type. He has published a five book science fiction series called 'Mineran', a children's diversity book and has a couple of unpublished novels waiting for an agent to find them worthy. When he is not

writing, Phil lives with his wife, high in the glorious Welsh hills.

Mair Dunlop

Mair is an enthusiastic member of our writing group writing under a pen name. So shrouded in mystery is she, that when she appears in the writing group she is nothing more than a wisp of smoke.

S W Fellows

Recently re-entering the world of writing, S W Fellows is learning so many exciting things. She enjoys composing poetry, but she also loves to write prose. She has completed a family story and is working on a murder mystery, so it's all systems go!

Fiona Knowles-Holland

Fiona Holland has written two novels, *Before All Else* and *Children of the Sky*. She won the Gladstone Library Prize for Short Fiction in 2013 and was runner up in the 2017 Carnival of Words Literature Festival. Her short story *Traffic* was published by the University of Chester Press as part of their Cheshire Prize for Literature Anthology, *Island Chain* in 2019. Fiona is a creative writing tutor and civil funeral celebrant.

Julie Huxley

Julie Huxley caught the writing bug at primary school when, to her surprise, the teacher read out

her treasure story. After raising her family, she took an English Literature degree. Reading and writing every day reignited her pleasure for telling stories and she is now a member of two writing groups, which provide invaluable encouragement and feedback. She continues to write and hopes to be published one day.

Catherine Jones

Catherine works in healthcare and has been enjoying being a part of the creative writing group for the past two years. When she is not in work or writing, she can usually be found in dangerous places chasing after her three 'spirited' children.

Peter Jones

Peter writes short stories and poetry, both of which he took up after retiring from teaching in further education. He has performed in North Wales, Liverpool and Chester in venues as varied as Llangollen Railway, community arts centres, pubs, libraries and theatres.

D M Kelly

D M Kelly is a shy unassuming writer who writes for personal enjoyment and not for fame and fortune. Writing under a nom de plume, she prefers to remain anonymous and maybe somewhat mysterious.

Eileen O'Reilly

Eileen mostly hides behind a computer screen in rural North East Wales. Sometimes she loiters in coffee shops, pretending she's not listening to the people at the next table. Eileen's stories and poems have been published in Riverbabble (USA), Writing Magazine (UK) and Pure Slush (Australia). She completed her debut novel, *Secrets*, in 2019.

David Powell

David is a self-employed carpet cleaner although he has had many different jobs. Until 10 years ago he hadn't written anything and would do anything to avoid the pen. David is dyslexic, however, having gone through a tough time in his life, for some reason he started to put his thoughts and troubles down in a notebook on his phone. These actions became a sort of therapeutic exercise, he believes, which worked well and some of his writing turned into poems which is how he discovered his love of writing.

Printed in Great Britain
by Amazon